AMANDA CARPENTER

Cry Wolf

Harlequin Books

TORONTO • NEW YORK • LONDON
AMSTERDAM • PARIS • SYDNEY • HAMBURG
STOCKHOLM • ATHENS • TOKYO • MILAN
MADRID • WARSAW • BUDAPEST • AUCKLAND

Harlequin Presents first edition October 1993
ISBN 0-373-11596-2

Original hardcover edition published in 1992
by Mills & Boon Limited

CRY WOLF

Printed in U.S.A.

"Don't ever try to provoke me again."

"Not even to clear the air?" she asked, insouciantly.

"My God," he uttered, "you need taming."

"Oh, I hope not," she retorted before she could help herself. *Did she mean it in taunting reply, or in fearful exclamation?* "But then I hear powerful men prefer docility."

He took a step toward her, his eyes two great, eruptive black pools as they focused on her soft, vulnerable mouth.

AMANDA CARPENTER, who wrote her first Harlequin romance when she was nineteen, was raised in South Bend, Indiana, but now lives in England. Amanda endeavors to enhance the quality of her romance novels with original story lines and an individual style. When she's not writing, she pursues her interests in art, music and fashion.

Books by Amanda Carpenter

HARLEQUIN PRESENTS

703—THE WALL
735—THE GREAT ESCAPE
759—RAGING PASSION
919—WAKING UP
991—ROSE-COLOURED LOVE
1047—RECKLESS
1127—THE GIFT OF HAPPINESS
1175—CAPRICE
1384—PASSAGE OF THE NIGHT

HARLEQUIN ROMANCE

2605—A DEEPER DIMENSION
2648—A DAMAGED TRUST

CHAPTER ONE

NIKKI ASHTON was running for her life when she stumbled around the corner of an old brick building and blundered headlong into the hard, unyielding wall of someone's chest.

They had caught her. There would be no second chance, nowhere else to run. As strong arms encircled her, Nikki screamed, a terrible lonely cry from a soul that had found its hell in utter hopelessness.

She was taken by the shoulders and shaken once, a hard, decisive gesture, before the man let go of her as if she bore some kind of contagious disease, and his mellifluous voice over her head cracked sharp as a steel-tipped whip, as hard as the hands that had held her, and as pitiless. 'Get a hold of yourself, woman! I'm not going to rape you, for God's sake. Bumping into you was an accident!'

Left without support, her legs collapsed underneath her, and she tumbled to the ground, but Nikki's head lifted. Whoever she had run into, it was not one of the two men who had dragged her down a dark alley and attacked her. Yellow light from a streetlamp halfway down the filthy block shone on her short black hair and gleamed on the high pale cheekbones of the small face, the great drowning pools of summer-blue eyes.

All she could see was a black towering figure, for the light came from behind him. He seemed to hesitate, but only for a moment. She reached desperately to pluck at the trousered leg so fleetingly close, but the material slipped agonisingly through fingers that could not curl to grasp it properly.

'Don't go——' she gasped, the harsh sound breaking from a parched throat, and perhaps it was just the rebirth of hope that had her imagining that the unidentifiable figure hesitated again. The same hope had tears destroying sight so that she dashed one hand across her face and left a wet, sticky trail. 'Please,' she whispered. 'I'm in trouble.'

That wet, sticky streak stood out like a beacon against the snow-white pallor of her face, for it was blood.

'Dear God,' said the man in a completely altered tone of voice. He squatted in front of her, and Nikki looked into a dark brown gaze that, when softened, would look like velvet, but now stabbed rapier-sharp. 'You're American, aren't you? What the hell are you doing in Soho at night? Don't you know, you witless creature, this is no place for a sightseeing trip on your own?'

'Does it look like I'm on a sightseeing trip?' she exploded in furious reaction, cradling her curled hands against her breast, for they were on fire. Since flight no longer seemed imperative, the pain had room to come back. 'I'm lost and two men are chasing me! There was one just behind me—that's why I ran around the corner so hard!'

The man rose to his feet and walked away. Stunned, Nikki bowed her dark head over her injured hands. The hope, then, had been for nothing.

But he had simply gone to the street corner, peered around it and strode back. He knelt and said, sounding brusque, 'There's no one there now, but we shouldn't stay here in case they come back. Are you hurt too badly to walk?'

In spite of his curt tone, the large hand that wiped the smear of blood from her face, then took hold of both of hers and turned them open, was very gentle indeed. She straightened her fingers as much as she could for his inspection, long, delicate fingers she had always kept neatly, had always cared for so well. The palm of each hand was slashed with a diagonal cut, from the base of the index finger to the opposite corner, and both were still bleeding.

The man drew in a quick breath, eyes widening with shock before they filled with a terrible fury. His hard brown gaze lifted to hers. 'They did this to you?'

'They tried to do worse!' she snapped, the embers of outrage flaring again to animate the delicate lines of her face. 'I grabbed the wrist of the one with the knife. When he yanked away, I did this to myself.'

One of his eyebrows lifted satirically at the sight of Nikki's sparkling blue eyes and aggressive, jutting chin, for, terrified or not, she looked ready to do battle all over again. 'We need the police and a doctor,' he said decisively. 'Let's get you to the nearest phone.'

He drew her to her feet, where she swayed unsteadily until he put one arm around her waist and helped her down the street, his lean athletic body brushing hers with each fluid stride. Nikki had recovered herself enough to notice details about him. His head was grey all over, a thick, vibrant pelt of iron hair like a wolf's.

The nearest phone happened to be in the stranger's car just two blocks down. Nikki stared wryly at the subdued elegant length of the black Jaguar as he fitted his key into the lock. The car suited the rolling, coiled grace of the tall man, but only as an accessory. This was not the kind of man who needed a status-symbol car to proclaim his worth to the world. This was a man who took quality and used it, but did not give it too much importance in his mind. She had known many men like that, and from long experience she knew power when she looked it in the face.

Her terror-induced adrenalin had receded but the resulting depression had not yet set in, so Nikki was remarkably clear-thinking, almost light-headed. When the grey-haired stranger turned to help her into the passenger-seat, she felt everything he did as separate and important in itself: the quick sensitivity of his dark eyes assessing her present condition, the long, graceful hand he extended that was saved from being willowy by the sheer breadth of physical strength across the palms, the tiny predatory shift of his lean, impassive face as he scanned the empty street one last time.

Understated, she thought, settling into the seat as he shut the door and moved to the driver's side. Restrained. Then she thought of the expression in his hard dark eyes as he had looked down on her poor hands. No, *leashed*.

As soon as he had got into the car, he pressed the automatic door locks. His startlingly grey head turned to her as the metallic bolts thunked into place, the ungentle gaze boring into hers. A card player's face, a boardroom face long familiar with power manoeuvres, and not as old as the grey hair might indicate; Nikki met his gaze with unfeigned composure.

'Don't you have even the slightest apprehension at being locked in a stranger's car?' he said sardonically.

Watch those hard eyes. Nikki pointed out with absolutely no trace of anger, 'I am alive. If I had not run into you, I might be dead now. That tends to put things into a certain perspective.'

'Perhaps you extend your trust too easily,' he said silkenly.

She gave him a tiny smile, then shaped her reply with a succinct baring of even white teeth. 'A case of the devil and the deep blue sea?'

There was still no facial change, but his gaze, locked with hers, undertook a subtle shift. Nikki's heart pounded once, hard. His eyes lowered, and as he lifted the white scarf from around his neck he said, 'Hold out your hands.'

No reassurances were forthcoming. For all she knew of him, he could be waiting to tie her up. Nikki was quite adept at reading nuances; she was to make of him what she would, and cope with her reactions in her own way. It was another key to the man. He had a certain amount of compassion, but it only went so far, and without so much as saying a word he was telling her what he must have said to many a business associate: deal with it or get out.

She smiled with genuine amusement. It lit her features, transforming her into a wise woman, and told him more clearly than anything else could have done that she saw through him and was not cowed. The last person able to do so had died five years ago, and not even she had possessed such a straight purity of gaze. This young woman was rare.

He took hold of the silk scarf with both hands and the broad shoulders underneath the black evening jacket flexed effortlessly. The fragile material tore, a tiny violent sound. Nikki held out her wounded hands in a gesture that was expressly vulnerable, and with great care he wrapped the ruined pieces of expensive silk around her palms.

Then he reached across her, an unexpected movement that made her blink with surprise as she shrank back instinctively in her seat, either to give him room or to avoid contact—she wasn't sure which. He grasped her seatbelt, pulled it cross her slight body and buckled her in. 'I wasn't aware that we intended to go anywhere,' she said with some acidity, and earned for herself a sidelong ironic glance.

'Maybe you might prefer sitting here for an hour or two until the police arrive, but, I assure you, I do not,' he informed her with a bored impatience. So sorry that I wasn't psychic enough to read your intentions, she murmured in silent sarcasm, for some reason piqued that he then proceeded to ignore her existence.

After fastening his own seatbelt and starting the car, he switched the car phone on to an intercom so that he could talk while driving, and he punched out a phone number on the lit display, while Nikki grimaced to herself and hunched down in her seat.

The Jaguar purred down the quiet side-street and merged with the Thursday night London traffic as the amplified tones of the telephone connection rang and rang. By the various electronic clicks Nikki knew that the call had been redirected twice before someone actually answered.

It was a man, and he sounded impatient. 'Yes?'

'Gordon,' said the grey-haired man beside her, who had been silent so long that she jumped. Unimpeachable British accent, she mused irrelevantly. Probably Etonian. 'Are you in London?'

'Yes.'

'Could you be at my town house in a half an hour?'

'If it's important.' The tone of the man on the other end of the phone had changed drastically, all impatience gone.

'Bring your medical bag.'

'Harper, are you all right?' The question came across sharply, and told Nikki a number of things. The man she sat beside was named Harper—Mr Harper?—and Gordon on the other end of the connection was not only a doctor, but a friend.

'Don't worry, I'm fine,' he said briefly. 'But I have someone with me who has hurt her hands, perhaps badly.'

'Give me twenty minutes.'

The man beside her broke off the connection just as they pulled up to the gaudy, iridescent light displays at Piccadilly Circus where traffic was snarled to nearly a standstill. Nikki had never seen it any other way and she looked around her with a lively interest.

Nikki used to think she had a fairly good sense of direction until she came to live in London, where all the streets twisted and curved and intersected at the queerest angles. It was because the city was so old. If she came out of the wrong exit from the Tube, she was reduced to searching for her bearings with the help of a dog-eared A to Z book of maps. She used to be charmed by the riotous maze of cobbled streets, but that confusion had nearly killed her tonight.

She had been close to Leicester Square, which had always seemed so safe because of the crowds from the nightclubs, the West End theatre-goers, the tourists, and the ever present black taxi cabs. Leicester Square was the immediate neighbour of Soho, where she had never dared to go, for though it was littered with restaurants it was also littered with drunks, prostitutes, porno nightclubs, and it was a very dangerous place to be at night for a young woman on her own.

The two men who had attacked her had worked as a team, driving her as if she were an animal into Soho's unplumbed depths.

Harper next called the police, explained the circumstances, and made arrangements for someone to meet them at his address near Berkeley Square in Mayfair. Aside from supplying her name when asked, Nikki remained silent throughout the exchange, bemused at the direction her life seemed to be taking without her volition, studying the man beside her with an almost dreamy fascination.

His dark glance shot over to her, swiftly and without warning, and caught her narrow-eyed perusal before she could mask it. His eyebrows raised almost imperceptibly. They were black, Nikki noticed, and sleek and arced just enough to lend a hint of unpredictability to an extremely handsome face.

Harper Beaumont.

His name didn't mean anything to her. But when he gave it to the police she heard the instant, utter respect in their response.

Her earlier impression was accurate, then. This was a very powerful man indeed.

One learned certain things when one stayed for any length of time in a city, and among them were which areas to avoid and where the rich lived. Nikki knew of the multimillion-pound mansions along Bishop's Avenue in Hampstead, the upper-class St John's Wood, trendy Chelsea. Then of course there was Mayfair, south of Oxford Street, west of Hyde Park, site of the American

Embassy and redolent with that psychic brush of power personified in the man beside her.

The Jaguar purred through the expensive neighbourhood like a cat on a midnight prowl, where the stone buildings were latticed with high black wrought-iron gates and the windows that glowed with golden light were shrouded in curtained privacy. One could smell politics from a mile off, she thought drily, and money. A lot of money. The car slowed and turned towards a basement garage, the door of which lifted in electronic silence, and they slid down into darkness.

'Stay where you are,' said Harper as he climbed out of the car. Grimacing, for she couldn't see a thing, Nikki did as she was told.

The basement garage flooded with light, revealing very neatly kept shelves and more room than she had expected, and Harper strode around the car to her side, opening the door and bending to unbuckle her seatbelt. 'Thank you,' she said drily as she climbed out of her seat.

He turned on his heel; this man had neat, precise movements that spoke not only of control, but a conservation of his energy and a universe made to order. But, she reflected, some men got too used to giving orders. She followed him up half a flight of stairs, through a door, and they were confronted by a small dark-haired man, impeccably dressed in a suit.

'Sir,' said the man with a slight bow.

'Duncan, we will shortly be having visitors. Ah, forgive me,' said Harper smoothly, 'we already have one. This is Nikki Ashton. See to her comfort, will you? Don't touch her hands, Dr Stanhope is coming. Er—Nikki, this is my man, Duncan Chang.'

So he was Eurasian, and, by his bowed greeting, more
Asian than European. Harper moved to one side and
she got her first full look at the small, neatly pro-
portioned man with sleek black hair, sallow, old ivory
skin, and the dark impassive eyes which had a slight tilt
but were not slanted. Duncan could have been twenty-
five, or forty-five.

She pressed her bandaged hands together, carefully,
as they throbbed, and inclined her head to him slightly,
in a very Western approximation of the Oriental courtesy,
and surprised the manservant into a smile of amused
delight. Harper's laser-beamed glance shot to the back
of her skull, sharp, imperious; she must have imagined
it, for he was turning to stride smoothly towards the front
lounge to leave her with Duncan Chang.

'If you would come with me, Miss Nikki,' murmured
the man who was of the same height as she, 'I shall fix
you a hot drink. Do you like tea?'

'Yes, both Indian and Chinese,' she replied as she followed him into a compact but excellently appointed
kitchen. Duncan indicated a chair at the small table in
one corner, and she settled herself as he whirled around
the kitchen with a dancer's grace. 'And please, I am just
Nikki.'

Very quickly the small task was accomplished. Duncan
asked, 'Shall I, as the English say, play Mother for you?'

Nikki nodded and replied, 'Yes, please. Milk, one
sugar. Tell me, did you happen to learn English in
Canada?'

Again Duncan smiled as he set a steaming cup of tea
in front of her; only later was she to find out how rare
that was. He told her, 'My father was Canadian, my
mother from Peking. Living in England as I now do, it

makes me somewhat a patchwork quilt, don't you think?'

Patchwork quilt, yes. Just as she was patchwork, comprised of the many places she had been to. But the strength of will that sewed her together was now unravelling raggedly at the seams. The depressing come-down from adrenalin and the distressing events of the evening hit with heavy suddenness. Nikki bowed her head and hid her eyes in one bandaged hand.

The kindness in Duncan Chang's voice nearly undid her. 'You are in pain, yes? I would offer you aspirin, but Dr Stanhope will soon be here and shall undoubtedly wish to give you something else.'

She had control, at least, of her voice. 'Yes, I know, but thank you for the thought.'

The front doorbell went, a muted sound coming over the small intercom by the kitchen door. The manservant pressed a button, and a voice she recognised from the car phone said, with all the impatience back in abundance, 'Gordon here. Let me in, Duncan.'

'Certainly, Dr Stanhope. Will you excuse me, Miss Nikki?'

'Certainly, Mr Duncan,' she said, taking a very gentle revenge for his persistent usage of 'Miss', and she was rewarded with the sight of a grin that was smothered hastily before the manservant left her alone in the kitchen.

Her body felt strung out from the various reactions she had gone through in the last hour and a half, muscles like toffee that had been pulled too thin. Only two hours ago she had started her way home from the cinema at Leicester Square to her roomy bed-sit in Knightsbridge without an inkling of the terror and the pain to come, without the slightest premonition of this place or these people.

The experience could have been far more traumatic than it was, except that Nikki had a tough streak of independence that her small-boned exterior masked to the casual observer. She was already mentally adjusting, reaching underneath the ragged edges of exhaustion for a wellspring of endurance.

Besides, there was a calm, affluent elegance to this house that she recognised and could relax in. Though she had never seen this place before, some aspects of it reminded her of her childhood, a golden age of remembrance where the world was a safe one made of small, simple pleasures.

Having found her equilibrium, Nikki turned her mind to a mental game she had played almost all her life, that of assessing what other people were and what they would do, not realising that this too was from her past, a characteristic she had learned from the clever adults who had surrounded her.

Gordon Stanhope would insist on seeing Harper Beaumont first, to get explanations and reassure himself that his friend was indeed unhurt. Harper Beaumont would not be in the habit of explaining much—his eyes were too full of secrets—but he would advise his doctor friend to see what information he could get from Nikki, for the habit of acquiring information was strong in powerful people.

Harper Beaumont would be a quick, concise puppet-master, sitting back and waiting while events moved to his choreography, more efficient than most she had known, and Duncan Chang would lead the doctor back here in—she glanced at a wall clock—less than two minutes now.

She was right and she was wrong. The kitchen door opened on time, but not on Duncan. It revealed the large, silent-moving puppetmaster himself, with a slim, elegant blond man following behind who carried a doctor's bag.

Harper Beaumont appointed himself as audience by leaning back against the kitchen counter in front of the microwave, arms crossed over a massive chest, lean face attentive and so inscrutable that the Chinese could have taken lessons from him. Nikki's pulse-rate increased so gently that she almost didn't notice it. Harper did not perform introductions but left the other two to react to each other unassisted, so Nikki looked up into sparkling grey eyes and said with a crooked smile, 'Dr Stanhope, I presume.'

'Just so, my dear,' replied the elegant man, who deposited his bag on the table and opened it. He was youngish, around thirty-three or -four, with the polished air of a man who enjoyed an ascendant career and a sophisticated lifestyle. 'And you are Nikki. Now, hold out your hands and let me see the reason why I had to abandon such a delicious salmon mousse.'

His profession was one in which such interruptions were a way of life, but that barely restrained impatience she had noticed over the phone was still present, adding a delicate resentful bite to the light words.

The woman must have been very attractive. Nikki held out her blood-stained, bandaged hands, which Gordon began to unwrap swiftly while she murmured, 'Mr Beaumont interrupted your supper? Perhaps if you hurry you might be on time for what's offered as dessert.'

The sexual implication was subtly made but obvious, and Nikki saw by his reaction that her guess was quite accurate. Gordon paused, his startled grey eyes lifting to hers in sharp reassessment while Harper chuckled, a surprisingly warm sound, and said, 'I warned you, Gordon. And watch yourself; she doesn't read expressions. She reads the eyes.'

She shouldn't have been quite so surprised at having herself so accurately read, but it had after all been a while since she'd been around such penetrating intelligence. After a moment Gordon's gaze became amused as he ran it from the tousled, shining black hair cut short around her feminine-shaped head, the delicate, almost childlike bone-structure of her solemn face, the very blue eyes, the long neck as graceful as a swan's, and the composed posture of her small body.

Her clothes were non-committal, being simple American jeans, tennis shoes, and an attractive loose blouse. A single gold necklace lay along the curves and hollows of her collarbones, tastefully plain but expensive. She looked barely sixteen, and the doctor had accepted that first impression almost automatically. As he looked again, however, with a trained, observant gaze, he found the enigma that Harper had discovered almost at once. She *was* young and yet not, for her poise was too old for a teenager, her self-imposed endurance that of an experienced adult, and her summer-blue, sky-wide eyes looked as if they could take apart a man's body and find his soul.

And there were unusual lines of pain on either side of her curved mouth. The doctor in Gordon resurfaced and he bent his attention to swiftly unwrapping her hands and staring at her wounded palms. 'What an inconvenient place to hurt oneself,' the blond man said reflectively. 'But thankfully there won't be permanent damage. Are you up to date on your tetanus jabs?'

She nodded, her blue eyes intently fixed on Harper, who knew that she didn't see him at all.

'I think no stitches are necessary, but you'll be in some discomfort if you don't manage to keep your hands as immobile as possible until the cuts have a chance to close over.' In the midst of cleaning the wounds, he glanced at her stiff expression. 'This will, of course, be difficult.'

'Yes.' Pain made her reply terse.

Gordon asked then, with a gentleness unusual for him, 'Do you have any family that you can stay with for a time, to make things easier for you?'

Harper was silent, always watching. Nikki felt his presence as intensely as if he had reached out and touched her face. Her gaze focused on him with returning awareness, and then she looked away. 'Don't worry, I can manage.'

'That wasn't exactly an answer to his question, was it?' said Harper with pointed dryness, his hard dark gaze on her. There was about him the quiet of one who could wait years for an answer if need be, an indomitable patience.

'I believe it's none of your business,' replied Nikki with a flash of stern admonishment, as she instantly, totally rejected the attempt to pry into her life. The blond man beside her sucked in his breath while Harper's expression darkened. She didn't need to be told any louder that it had been a very long time since anyone had presumed to talk back to him. How would he react? she wondered, staring at him in almost clinical fascination.

'You do, of course, know best,' said Harper with chilly, sardonic politeness as he inclined his grey wolf's head. How old was he? Thirties, forties? The body was athletic, the hair grey, the face lined at the corners of eyes and mouth, but with character, not age.

'I do know how well the English can freeze one out while murmuring civilities.' She could not have expressed even to herself why she chose to attack, unless it was, perhaps, something to do with his cold demeanour which was at such odds with the vitality in his face. Nikki's summer-blue eyes met his, and clashed, and she said quietly, 'I am not stupid. Don't patronise me.'

The cutting harshness faded from Harper's face and he smiled at her smokily, as sudden and as astonishing as the warm humanity in his laughter. He had a singularly devastating smile. Harper said strangely, 'I should know better than that, shouldn't I?'

Nikki had pause to mull over that curious reply as two policemen arrived, and Harper went out to talk with them. Meanwhile Gordon recovered himself and finished cleaning and dressing her wounds, evidently much amused by the clash between Nikki and Harper, for he laughed soundlessly the whole time.

The antiseptic he used was painful enough to bring tears to her eyes.

'All done,' said Gordon as he finished quickly. Nikki released a pent-up breath, thanked him in a shaky voice, and gratefully swallowed the pain-killers he gave her with the remainder of her cooling tea.

'You'll want to join Harper and the police now that I've had my wicked way with you,' said Gordon. 'I'm sure they're ready to question you now.'

'Thank you for all your help. And I am sorry about your interrupted supper,' Nikki couldn't help refrain from saying, a furtive devil peeping out of her blue eyes.

The blond man grinned a remarkably mischievous grin. He replied in dulcet tones, 'Quite all right, my dear. Dessert has only a—limited fascination, while I wouldn't have missed coming here tonight for the world.'

She raised her eyebrows at his cryptic words, but went on, 'You can send a bill for the housecall to me, in care of Peter Bellis Marketing Limited.'

'My love,' Gordon murmured, laughing as he brought his nose close to hers, 'you couldn't afford me.'

Nikki's eyes smiled back. 'You make too many snap judgements.'

The kitchen door settled into place. She and Gordon had been so caught up in their exchange that they hadn't noticed Harper's silent arrival. Nikki tore her attention away from the slim blond man, met Harper's gaze, and felt the force of that impact down to her toes. If she had not already been sitting down, she might have lost her balance in sheer surprise.

The card player's face had cracked for once and what showed underneath the façade was—intense irritation.

Gordon, however, remained manifestly unaffected. If anything, his smile broadened. Harper looked at the doctor, and a tiny muscle moved in his lean jaw, but his voice was amazingly nonchalant, even insolent, as he said, 'You can let yourself out, can't you, Gordon?'

'Thank you, Gordon. Goodnight, Gordon,' said the blond man, not a whit put out by his friend's rudeness. His shoulders shook mirthfully as he gathered up his doctor's bag and paused to stroke her cheek with one impudent forefinger. 'Ah, Nikki. It was well worth skipping dessert for this.'

Nikki's eyes narrowed sharply as the blond man took his leave. Something had indeed happened, and she hadn't missed it. She just hadn't understood, but she didn't doubt for a moment that both Gordon and Harper had.

CHAPTER TWO

NIKKI wasn't allowed much time to puzzle over the curious exchange between Harper and Gordon, however, for as the door closed on the doctor's exit Harper turned and strolled over to where she sat. It took a conscious act of will for her to keep from shrinking away from the warm hand that came under her chin to tilt her face up, since certainly he was no closer than Gordon had been when the doctor had tended to her hands.

The kitchen light was far too bright and somewhat fuzzy. She blinked rapidly in an effort to bring Harper's intent, obscure expression into focus, unaware that her eyes had dilated to the extent that the blue was almost entirely submerged by the over-bright black pupils in a pointed, delicate face that had gone white with exhaustion and delayed stress.

Nikki submitted docilely to Harper's practical and sensitive offer to wash her face. The cool flannel was refreshing, his long fingers so soothing that she unconsciously sighed in pleasure. It helped to restore her flagging energy so that when she followed him down the hall and towards the front lounge she was feeling almost normal.

The lounge was an elegant place, with cream leather sofas, indirect lighting, very dark inlaid wood furniture and, she was interested to note, a well-polished baby grand piano tucked to one side. Her educated gaze ran consideringly over the few pieces of original artwork around the spacious room: one painting was nineteenth-

22

century French; another framed picture was a Dali sketch; and the third was a Dutch watercolour by an artist she was unfamiliar with. They were a rather strange mixture that blended surprisingly well, which was a credit to the mind that had matched them together in one room.

Then she saw the truly magnificent Chinese silk screen in one corner and her face lit up. Harper, who watched her expression as soon as she appeared in the room, smiled to himself to see the frankly covetous approval that shone out of her eyes before she recovered herself and turned to greet the two inspectors, one man and one woman, who had risen to their feet.

After ascertaining the extent of her injuries, the policewoman asked the majority of the questions. Nikki found that she was intensely grateful for the other woman's professional blend of brisk methodology and gentleness. She answered as well as she could, but unfortunately she wasn't able to tell the police very much. The two men had grabbed her from behind as she had walked past an open alleyway, and she had never got more than a flashing glimpse of their shadowed faces before she had managed to get away. Their clothing had been nondescript as well; indeed, the only thing she could remember with any clarity was the one who had been behind her as he held her arms and whispered hoarse obscenities in her ear.

Nikki broke off at that point, shuddering as a mask of distaste distorted her features. She didn't need the policewoman's grave assurance to tell her how lucky she'd been. Harper had sat the entire time in one corner, a silent, impassive listener, the brown eyes hooded. He had shed his black evening jacket and tie, and his white shirt and tailored black trousers were an unsoftened spotlight in the muted pastel creams of the room.

Eventually the policeman, who had primarily taken notes, sighed and asked one last question. 'And there is absolutely nothing else you can think of?'

She shook her head with regret. 'I'm sorry. Even if I had the use of my hands, I wouldn't be able to offer you a decent sketch of them. I just didn't get the chance to see them well enough.'

Harper spoke for the first time since she had entered the lounge, his deep voice musical in comparison with the policeman's gruffness. 'You are an artist?'

Nikki shrugged and struggled to control a yawn. 'Of a sort. I do free-lance design for a marketing company in Knightsbridge, anything from posters and letter-head logos to television sets for advertisements.'

'Any good?' he asked carelessly.

'Well, of course,' replied Nikki as her slim dark brows shot up, as if surprised that anyone would even think to question the quality of her work.

'Well,' said the policewoman, who rose to her feet, as did her partner, 'we'll be in touch if we find anything out. Please contact us if you happen to remember anything else.'

Nikki nodded from where she sat on the couch. She was hunched forward with her elbows on her knees, and while she felt that she probably should say something else her brief spurt of energy had rapidly deserted her. She rubbed her tired face with the backs of her bandaged hands while Harper saw the police out the front door.

She felt as if she were wrapped in cotton wool. It wasn't pleasant. Two long muscular legs came into her line of view, then bent as Harper squatted, his hard brown eyes watching her from the concealment of lazy lids.

Inconsequentially, she said, 'I've disrupted your entire evening.'

He raised one long-fingered hand while the firmly held mouth relaxed into a faint smile, as he said, lightly dismissive, 'It had become, in any event, an abysmal bore.'

It seemed to her that he was being far too gracious about the whole thing; it wasn't in character. She would tell him so in a minute. She frowned fiercely and said, 'I feel very odd.'

Oh, there was a hard-edged grin. That was more like it. He said drily, 'That's because you're drugged to the eyeballs. Whatever did Gordon give you anyway?'

'Dunno. Thought it was aspirin, or something.' This time she couldn't contain the wide yawn that cracked her jaw, and afterwards she blinked at Harper in groggy dismay. 'I've got to go home!'

'You'll spend what's left of the night here, of course,' he told her. Was that resignation in his voice? But he was still smiling. 'I had Duncan make up a bed for you before he retired for the night.'

She considered that, and was appalled. 'No, you really must take me home now.'

His broad shoulder moved under her cheek. Now he was laughing at her; Nikki battled against the encroaching darkness with all her remaining strength. It was important that she understand just what was going on. Harper said quietly, as he carried her slight weight up the stairs, 'I'm not taking you anywhere. Do you have any idea what time it is?'

She sighed and turned her nose into his shirt. His warm scent flooded her senses, and she breathed deep with the surprising pleasure. 'Then call me a cab,' she murmured, eyes closed. 'Because I'm not staying here.'

'Yes, you are.' He laid her down on something, eased off her tennis shoes and unzipped her jeans.

That opened her eyes. Nikki made a herculean effort and sat up, hazily taking in the shadowed room and the large dark figure bent over her. 'No, I can't,' she said.

Harper restrained her weak protests with ease. 'You must.' Her jeans were replaced by warm bedcovers.

Oh, my. She'd have to remember to argue about it in the morning. In the meantime, he was so incredibly gentle, and the bed was so soft. She leaned forward and pressed her lips against his lean cheek as he urged her down to the pillows, and murmured, 'Thank you for saving my life.'

He turned his head towards her kiss so that his stern male mouth connected with hers and softened. 'Go to sleep,' he whispered, but she already had.

Nikki opened her eyes and was wide awake all at once, body rigid, head pounding, terrified as she stared at a darkened, unfamiliar room until realisation flooded over her and she almost groaned aloud.

She never could sleep well in a strange bed, and had always envied those who could rest wherever they lay down. Perhaps that had been what awakened her; certainly the drug Gordon had given her had worn off, for her hands throbbed when she flexed them, and her mouth was hot and dry from the aftermath.

She was obviously in a guest room. What she could see of it from some pale, unidentifiable illumination was tasteful and as impersonal as a hotel room. The luminous digital clock on the bedside table said that it was half-past·five.

Nikki slid out of the bed, a servant to some great imperative, and fumbled for her jeans which were lying neatly on the floor. Her money and keys were still in the pockets; with extreme difficulty she managed to wriggle into them and get the zip up. She sat, panting slightly, to stuff her feet into her tennis shoes.

Damn, damn, damn. The doctor had been right, of course. Some amount of movement was necessary but excruciating, and she could feel the cuts break open and start to bleed again.

The town house was so silent. Carefully Nikki eased into the hall and towards the stairs. She had to pass another dark room to get to them; she didn't know why she stopped, turned aside and glided soundlessly over the carpet to peer within the open door.

The figure in the bed was so very still. Nikki crept over to the side of the bed and stood for long moments staring down at Harper's serene face.

The mane of his thick hair spilled from his forehead, scarcely darker than the pillow it rested on. A sheet tangled at lean hips; he was bare from the waist up, and there was a suggestion of a darker shadow on the wide, strong chest. One muscled arm was flung out straight, the other bent with the hand tucked under the pillow.

He was asleep. He was a stranger, and Nikki's heartbeat was a crazy thing.

She tiptoed out of the room and down the stairs. The pale illumination had come from a light left on in the kitchen, whose door was propped open. Duncan was not up yet either.

What an ungracious thing to do, she thought, as she found a pad of paper and a pen by the phone in the hall. It wouldn't have hurt her to endure until morning to thank Harper and Duncan Chang in person. She was quite willing to admit that she was behaving in a somewhat erratic fashion, as she gritted her teeth against

the pain, found a way to grip the pen and scrawled across
the top page in shaky letters, 'Thank you for everything.'

She left the note in the middle of the hall table and
fumbled through the locks on the front door. There was
no denying that she was over-reacting to the stresses of
the night before, but she needed to be home in the privacy
of her bed-sit just as soon as she could possibly get there,
and waking up alone in a strange place after such a night
was a cold and comfortless experience.

Besides, she did remember everything, and Harper had
been right of course—she'd been in no shape to go home
at all, though she'd done her best to fight it. How galling
to be an imposition on a man such as he.

She eased out of the house, shivering in the pre-dawn
air, totally unprepared for the sense of bereavement she
felt as the front door closed behind her on the briefest
of glimpses into another life—it was like a candle going
out in the dark. 'Nikki, Nikki,' she muttered darkly,
shaking her head as she jogged down the steps and across
the street, 'you're a proud and wilful soul.'

Perhaps it wasn't the true reason why she was running
away, but it comforted her to think so.

Upstairs in the town house Harper opened his eyes,
which were quite alert and contemplative.

With remarkable ease Nikki caught a taxi which took
her to Knightsbridge and pulled to a stop just outside
the little mews where she lived.

Her bed-sit was spacious and airy, the fourth-floor
attic of a building of flats. She had two huge skylights
that let in great quantities of natural light or a dizzying
panoramic view of the stars, both of which more than
made up for the exorbitant gas bills she had to pay for
her central heating. If fingers got cold, fingers couldn't
work.

Nikki spared a wry glance at the bandaged fingers that wouldn't be doing any work for a while, and moved slowly, awkwardly, to make herself a cup of tea. Now that she could unwind in her own precious space she would have preferred just going to bed and curling up under her covers to sleep the day away, but she had far too much to do. Considering how long it took her to make a cup of tea, she couldn't even afford the luxury of an hour in bed.

She managed to put the cup on a tray and carry it over to her couch, which was shoved back against the one wall not covered with bookshelves. She turned the telly on so that the morning news would help keep her awake, then settled back to drink her cup of milky tea.

Thank God her mother and brother lived on the other side of the Atlantic! Much as she loved them, Nikki felt as though she'd spent her whole life battling to live independently from her family's wealth and influence. If either one of them found out what had happened to her last night, she'd never hear the end of it—besides, as she did love them very much, she wouldn't want to put them through the anxiety they'd experience were they to hear of her attack.

Nikki checked her watch and groaned. She had to go into the office; she had a meeting with Peter, the owner and managing director of the marketing company, and she wasn't looking forward to telling him that she would be unable to meet her obligations for the next couple of weeks. Peter's business was small but highly successful, and she was his most popular designer.

Nikki performed, in her mind, a minor miracle. With plastic bags over her hands, she managed a shower of sorts without getting her bandages too damp. She dressed in an ankle-length black skirt and sleek boots, and an off-the-shoulder black velvet top, with long, tight-fitting sleeves and an equally snug-fitting bodice. She looked smart and stylish, the sobriety of the outfit broken by the extreme femininity of her exposed collarbones and neck. The only problem was her pale, drawn face and tousled hair, and by nine o'clock she was in the small local hairdressers at the crossroads of the main intersection near her bed-sit where she normally got her hair cut.

She was lucky, as Gemma, the girl who usually cut her hair, was free for half an hour, and more than willing to shampoo and blow-dry the short black locks into a layered profusion of shining wisps which lay lightly along the pronounced angle of Nikki's cheekbones and delicate blue-veined hollow of her temples. Then Gemma, excited and sympathetic for the story Nikki told her about how she'd cut her hands, offered to help with a little make-up, and stroked a skilful blend of bluish-grey shadow under Nikki's eyebrows, making her blue eyes seem larger, along with a touch of dusky red colour along her cheekbones, which did much to disguise the effects of her interrupted night.

By ten Nikki felt ready to meet whatever reaction would be facing her at Peter's, and she travelled by bus to the smartly decorated offices, which were buzzing as usual with a high-octane mixture of impending deadlines and a fast-paced turn-over of work.

A chorus of greetings were called out as Nikki manoeuvred her way through the busy ground floor, and she responded with a quick smile and wave. She didn't stop to chat with any of the staff as she normally would have done, however, but went directly to Peter's office. He was on the phone and she cooled her heels for a quarter of an hour, waiting outside until he had finished.

Peter's door finally opened and he came out to greet her. He was a whippet-thin man in his forties who could never seem to sit still, full to overflowing with nervous energy. Nikki found him likeable, but exhausting.

'Fantastic news!' Peter said. 'I've just been on the phone to a prospective client, who's very interested in your work, Nikki, my love. This could be big, very big. If we manage to bag this guy, both of our reputations would sky-rocket. He's coming in for a chat in a half an hour, so our meeting will have to be brief, but I'd like you to stick around until he gets here so that he can talk to you himself. OK with you?'

'That depends,' she said warily as she rose to her feet and followed him into his office. Decorating his walls were several large framed paintings, most of them her work, the originals of advertisement posters for Covent Garden operas, West End musicals, and one for a Tate Gallery exhibition from last year. The elegant, colourful pictures were all so familiar to her that she didn't spare them a second glance, but settled with an inward sigh into the seat opposite Peter's desk. 'You see, I have some rather bad news.'

Peter forsook his chair to perch on the corner of his desk, then his glance fell, and he froze. 'Good God, what have you done to your hands?'

'That's the bad news, I'm afraid,' she said wryly, as she looked down also with a grimace. She told him, briefly, what had happened to her the night before, and finished with, 'So you see, I won't be able to work for a few weeks. You'll have to find someone else to take over my projects that won't wait.'

'I thought my luck was too good this morning!' he groaned deeply, and raked both hands through his untidy hair. 'Now what am I going to do? I've got this new client coming in fifteen minutes, specifically asking for you as designer, and I've all but promised him that we could deliver whatever he wanted!'

'Well, can't you put him off for a few weeks?' Nikki asked, rubbing at the bridge of her nose tiredly. Normally she loved the fast-paced pressure and took pride in the popularity of her work, but today she felt sluggish, unable to cope with the demand. 'Anyway, it would have taken me that long to finish the work I've already got. He wouldn't be losing out.'

'I was already counting on getting the other designers to do what you've got at the moment, so that you could concentrate on this project.' He looked at her helplessly. 'Forgive me for asking, but are you sure you can't do any work?'

She gave an angry-sounding little laugh and spread out her half-curled, bandaged hands. 'There's nothing wrong with my brain, Peter. But I'm afraid that any artwork is out of the question. I couldn't even wash my own hair or put on any make-up this morning; I had to stop at a hairdressers on the way.'

'Damn,' he swore softly.

'Look, I'll hang around,' she said, taking pity on him. 'Surely if I meet this guy and talk to him myself, he'll be reasonable about waiting. We won't lose this account if I can help it—that is, if he's as important as you say he is.'

'Oh, he is, darling,' she was assured fervently. 'A *very* important man. He's practically a British institution in himself—financial wizard, international entrepreneur, multi-millionaire, comes from a prominent family. Not only does he advise governments from time to time, but he's also one of the most prominent art collectors in the country, and all by the age of thirty-six. At one time all he had to do was appear at a private exhibition to establish an artist's reputation, but he's very elusive and hasn't been seen at an art gallery for five years now. Do you see why it's so vital to keep his business, if we can get it?'

She did, indeed. If they could win the business of a man of that calibre, not only did it mean possible international exposure for Peter's marketing firm, but it also meant a watershed for her own career. Intense frustration welled up so strongly that her hands started to tighten into fists until a sharp sear of pain brought a muffled exclamation from her.

'Don't worry, Peter,' she said grimly as he shot a sharp, enquiring glance at her. 'We'll work something out. Just how, I don't know, but we will.'

His buzzer on the desk sounded, and he answered it impatiently. It was his eleven o'clock appointment, and Peter straightened from the desk and attempted to smooth down his unruly thatch of hair. 'Bring him in, please,' he said to his secretary, and as they waited he whispered, 'Showtime, Nikki.'

The door opened, and Nikki's gaze swivelled to it and stopped. Everything stopped.

Peter stepped forward, hand outstretched to the man who had stridden into the office. 'How do you do? I'm Peter Bellis,' he said smoothly. 'And this is the designer we talked about over the phone—Nikki Ashton. Nikki, meet Harper Beaumont.'

'What?' she murmured, not really hearing, still in the grip of shock and surprised excitement. She could not tear her eyes away from him. He shook Peter's hand courteously yet somehow managed to hold himself aloof, clad in a formal, conservative dark blue suit, his hard, lean expression one of thorough boredom until his dark eyes met hers and flared alight, with something not quite a laugh, not quite a smile, but which sizzled electrically throughout her entire body.

If she had not already been sitting, she would have then, hard. This man did nasty things to her equilibrium. Peter threw her an exasperated glance. 'I said, this is Harper Beaumont——'

'Don't bother,' murmured Nikki dreamily, 'we've met.'

Peter's mouth fell open in surprise. Harper was watching her closely with a faint smile, while she strove very hard to maintain a composed expression. Underneath she was trembling from head to foot, when he hadn't even so much as said a word to her. What a ridiculous fool she was, what a ridiculous, naïve fool not to have recognised the electric current between them last night for what it really was. She didn't want to feel this kind of attraction for any man, let alone this vibrant, intense sexual voltage. It was both frightening and disturbing, and just what in the world was she supposed to do now?

She felt, against all sense or reason, an incredible urge to run over to Harper Beaumont and throw her arms around his waist in delighted welcome. How impossible, how absurd, what a haughty, repellent surprise he would show at such an uncontrolled gesture, and how inexplicably miserable she felt at quelling the urge.

'You look tired,' said Harper silkenly, ignoring the incredulous fascination of the man standing beside him.

'Delayed reaction,' she replied in a wry voice, furiously willing the tide of colour away from her face. Wretched man, to remind her of how she cravenly ran from his house. Without taking her eyes away from Harper's face, she explained to Peter, 'Harper was the man I bumped into last night in Soho. He took me back to his place, and called a doctor and the police. I—don't know what I would have done without him.'

'I see,' said Peter, which of course he didn't. 'Well, at least that takes care of one issue. You'll already know that Nikki is unable to take on new assignments for the next few weeks, but I'm sure that once you've looked at the quality of her work you'll agree that it's more than worth the wait.'

Harper turned his grey head and said softly, 'That remains to be seen.'

Nikki recoiled, her expression swiftly changing into one of haughty affront, but Peter just nodded and smiled and replied, 'Of course. Now if you can tell me what you want, I'll be happy to show you around the offices so that you can see what sort of things we can provide.'

For the next forty-five minutes the two men talked, while Nikki sat back and bore silent witness, alternately seething for how completely she was ignored, offended at Harper's earlier dismissal of her work, and feeling a fugitive sense of abandonment for what appeared to her to be a total rejection of whatever connection they had established last night.

Which was stupid. More than stupid, irrational, she told herself, inwardly struggling with the chaos her emotions were in. Of course any former personal contact would have nothing to do with the business of the day. He was far too successful; *she* was too successful to conduct her profession on that level. Besides, what did they really have established, anyway? Nothing, nothing at all—a chance meeting, and a display of common decency for someone in distress. That was over with, finished, kaput. A closed chapter. If it were not for the business at hand, they might never have met again.

Nothing of her inner turmoil showed on her delicate, calm face. Indeed, she looked withdrawn to the point of coldness, blue eyes watching both men analytically as they talked. Peter's energetic restlessness looked somehow sloppy and unrestrained next to Harper's relaxed body and contained dynamism. Every action, every nuance in his voice and body was a controlled output. The sheer power of personality he commanded was meticulously aimed and hit its mark time and again, never overshooting, never reaching overkill; how dangerous he was. In fact, she was quite sure Peter did not understand just how much. This man, unleashed and rampant, could destroy a person.

He was looking for an exclusive range of updated material for his own company, from new letter-heads to glossy booklets and magazines, even down to the design in his own City offices. Everything had to be co-ordinated. The targeted market was not the general public, but was very high indeed: bank managers, boards of directors, even governmental offices. Harper's own international clientele was cosmopolitan, sophisticated and extremely wealthy. They had expensive tastes and lifestyles, and a daunting level of expectation; in fact, Harper considered the matter so important that it warranted his personal attention, instead of being delegated down to some other department.

She could see Peter becoming more and more awed as the meeting went on, but Nikki had been brought up in just such an atmosphere of global connections and her mind was already racing ahead, anticipating each consideration before Harper ever mentioned it.

Then it was Peter's turn to present what he thought his company could provide, and by that time Harper had set him up so cleverly that the man was falling over himself in an effort to procure Harper's business. Nikki, her expression very wry, declined to go on the grand tour of the offices with the other two but instead had coffee with Peter's secretary as she waited for their return.

She refused to fall into the intelligent pitfall Harper had constructed. Though inwardly she was as much a victim as Peter and longed to be given the job, she would not scramble for it. Pride forbade it, especially after the cool way Harper had responded to Peter's high opinion of her work. Nikki had studied in Paris for seven years, first at a private boarding-school, then later at art school. She had been trained by the very best, and knew just what she was capable of. What she was not used to was having her work dismissed so cavalierly, not even by a renowned art collector. If he wanted her to do the job, he would have to ask her himself.

The sound of their voices echoed down the corridor, and Nikki turned her head. With every appearance of aplomb, she met Harper's shrewd, dissecting gaze, then set aside her coffee-cup and stood. 'Well?' she asked.

A faint, disturbingly enigmatic smile deepened the corners of Harper's stern mouth, but it was Peter who said, 'I'll leave you two to talk alone, shall I? Feel free to use my office.'

Nikki nodded and moved with careful grace to the closed door. So far, so good. It looked as if Harper was interested enough to make some kind of offer.

'Allow me,' said Harper, in a murmur as velvet as the top she wore, and one of his beautiful hands came over hers to grasp the doorknob.

Nikki's world rocked at the contact. She would have backed away from it, but the slight brush of clothing along her bare shoulder told her he was right behind her. He twisted the knob and gave it a gentle push so that it swung open to the empty room, and he followed as she entered.

She ignored the chairs, indeed noticed nothing of the office, as she swung around slowly to face him, her limbs so sluggish and heavy that she felt as if she swam very deep waters. 'You're a wicked man to wind Peter up the way you have,' she scolded, taking refuge in attack.

One eyebrow lifted, slow and satanic. 'Tactics and manoeuvres,' he said. Oh, yes, the puppetmaster was in fine form. 'Didn't you sleep well, darling?'

Damn her fine skin; the heat rose again to her cheeks. She murmured, 'I fought it every step of the way. But then you should know, shouldn't you?'

'What an argumentative creature you are, ready to do battle with the world. One wonders why you felt the need to run off the way you did,' he murmured. Never taking his eyes away from her face, he began to circle around the chair almost in front of her, leisurely, patiently beginning his stalk.

Nikki's breathing was severely restricted; she felt the same panic from early this morning tremble through her body and only hoped it wasn't visible. 'I didn't run away,' she replied—so casually! What a liar she was. 'I'd had an upsetting evening, woke up with a headache and wanted to go home. But you wouldn't take me when I asked.'

'Very unreasonable of me, I know,' he said ironically. He was at the back of the chair now. 'Especially when you were falling asleep in my arms. Instead I tucked you into bed—I don't know what came over me!'

'I told you—you're a wicked man who doesn't play fair.' She managed that with an admirable show of serenity.

'So I don't,' he murmured. Now he was past the chair and circling another one. 'You've got lovely legs.'

Nikki's eyes narrowed, and she said maliciously, 'I looked in on you when you were sleeping before I left.'

'I wasn't sleeping,' he said lazily.

Nikki's composure broke, and she whirled away, almost immediately trying to cover the retreat by running an idle finger along the edge of Peter's desk. But she didn't stop until the length of it was between them, and only then turned back to look at him. Her blue gaze made contact with dark, somewhat quizzical eyes, and she said the first thing that came into her mind. 'I didn't think we'd see each other again.'

Harper smiled a little, and with a deep-seated tremor she wondered what she had just revealed. God, but why bother trying to hide anything from that worldly, penetrating stare? He was too mature, too sophisticated, and, just as he'd done last night, he read her like a book. 'To be sure,' he said, 'I almost didn't recognise you.'

She laughed and recovered her composure somewhat. 'I'm not surprised,' she told him ruefully, and gestured down at herself. 'This professional image is quite a bit different from the ragged person you met last night.'

'I thought you recovered quite well,' he replied, turning to study the various framed pictures with a slight frown. Nikki tried to ignore the nervous butterflies in her stomach that fluttered as he paused by one of the striking paintings. It was hers. It was silly of her, but having him study her work made her feel like an insecure teenager again, brought to her tutor's attention. He sent her a sidelong glance. 'Any lasting effects?'

The grey hair at the back of his head curled over the collar of his suit, an intriguing contradiction in sensuality, for the steely colour belied the luxurious abundance. What would it feel like? She stopped the train of thought abruptly. She didn't want to know.

'Not a one,' she lied cheerfully. 'Unless, of course, you want to count the physical. What a coincidence you came here today.'

He laughed so softly that Nikki's heart shook within her. 'My dear,' drawled Harper as he turned back to face her, 'I never do anything by coincidence. Gordon sends his love but he wouldn't send a bill, although when I tell him how well you're doing he just might change his mind. What a precocious thing you are.'

That careless statement pierced straight through her, and she stiffened against it. 'Precocious?' she mocked, moving to lean against the desk. 'Why, thank you. I haven't been called that for years.'

'But you are,' he said, his eyebrows lifting smoothly. 'Many designers are in their thirties before they reach the level of success you enjoy, and what are you—twenty-two, twenty-three?'

'Twenty-four,' she replied, her eyes very bland. 'Why, how old are you?'

The hard, dark eyes lit with laughter. '*Touché*,' he murmured, 'I'm thirty-six, and yes, I have worn the label myself and know how tiresome it can become.'

Again she blurted out where her thoughts led her, without artifice or subterfuge. 'Why did you come?'

'Why?' he echoed, almost as if he had not considered the reasons, or as if he couldn't believe she did not see them for herself. 'To see what kind of images the woman I met last night would produce. To see how she would transform the perceptions she gleaned from other people's eyes, to see the person who surprised my very reserved Duncan into rare delight, and bewitched Gordon away from a midnight tryst he had spent months trying to set up. I came to see if you were as good as you so arrogantly thought you were.'

'I know my own worth,' she said coolly, flinging back her head in a proud gesture.

'You are mistaken,' said Harper with clinical, debilitating dispassion. 'You are not good.'

She drew in a deep breath, eyes brilliant and bewildered. He played her like his namesake, the harp, plucking strings she didn't comprehend, building an intimacy of understanding between them with such careless ease. The curve of Nikki's mouth began to tremble, and she turned away from him for she would not let him see it. No, she didn't comprehend what he was able to inflict by just the casual use of words. She didn't know if she felt a strange kind of grief or just astonishment, but she did know that he was destroying her composure systematically, for the full knowledge and intent of what he did were in those wise, ruthless eyes, and she might never forgive him for it.

'You are passionately superb,' he continued relentlessly, and her hands shook as she clasped them to her. 'You are sensitive without too much delicacy, subtle without being insipid, gloriously alive with colour, and expression, and your pictures have a fathomless depth. By the time you have matured into your vast talent, you will be quite breathtaking. Have you never considered how you are wasting yourself with this kind of throwaway art?'

'That's a purist attitude. I'm not the kind of artist to forsake the world for the privilege of starving in a garret,' she said, numbed, tumbled inside out by his inexplicable, softly spoken, terrible assault. 'These——' she gestured around the room '—these are real issues, and real people see them.'

His eyes gleamed like old copper. 'They are here today and gone tomorrow—why have you never painted for yourself?'

She gasped, her exposed throat moving on the tiny escape of breath at his own presumption, his own arrogance, and then she gave him his own brutal honesty back. 'Why do you hold yourself so compulsively aloof? Why does Gordon Stanhope never settle into stillness, but Duncan Chang carries inside him a bottomless pool of it? If you start asking questions like that, you should be sure you want to hear the answer.'

Harper walked to her, the muscular, predatory body moving to some fluid purpose, and he cupped her averted cheek in the palm of one large hand as he said strangely, 'But why else would I ask, Nikki? Of course I want to hear the answer.'

She didn't want his wisdom, or his terrible insight, and she didn't want this wretched desire for his hand to continue touching her. She turned her head and stabbed him with angry eyes. 'I told you once before, don't patronise me.'

'Is the truth patronising?' he countered lazily, his hand falling from her face only to land with shattering intimacy on the naked skin of her shoulder. Her knees nearly collapsed under its feather-light weight. His fingers tightened on her when she would have pulled back, holding her to that position of skin on skin between them, demanding, as his gaze demanded of hers, a continued communication. 'You are right, but only in part, for I am not always so compulsively aloof.'

What was this tense conversation—an argument, an outright fight, an agreement of some sort that she couldn't comprehend? Why did she feel like screaming at him, or breaking into tears, and why did she instead settle on some kind of explanation so that he would understand her?

'I pay a price for what I do; don't we all?' she whispered tautly. 'Maybe I don't paint for myself because people wouldn't be interested. Now, as it is, at least I can pay my bills by doing the one thing that gives me pleasure. I don't get weary, or disillusioned, or bored. Nothing else holds me the way my work does; it is the only thing in the world I can lose myself in.' -

'So you do it frantically, furiously. No wonder you're as far along in your career as you are. Of course it's the only thing in the world because it's the only thing you will let yourself be lost in. What an innocent you are,' said Harper, and he bent his head.

CHAPTER THREE

Nikki immediately saw Harper's intention and underneath the unrelenting pressure of his hand her body stiffened in frozen, resisting panic. Perhaps he felt it, for his fingers tightened even further. But perhaps he didn't, for with slow deliberation he continued to lower his mouth until those devastating male lips brushed hers.

She held herself too tightly and her tension broke into uncontrollable tremors, the panic swamping her so that she couldn't think or breathe, but the very consistency of the gentle, uncomplicated pressure from his mouth soothed her. He did not demand; indeed he did not even move until the trembling in her body eased somewhat and she gave a little unconscious sigh of relief.

This was not passion. This was some kind of salutation, as if Harper recognised and greeted her for what she really was. Either that, or it was some kind of tender farewell to—to what? Was this goodbye? That possibility sizzled through her with the swiftness of a lightning bolt, followed by the thunderous rumble of disappointment.

He had meant goodbye with his kiss. He had come, mingling personal curiosity with professional necessity, an astounding gesture from such an important, aloof man; but, for whatever reason, he must have decided to take his business elsewhere, and now he would turn and walk right out of her life, this time for good.

Harper drew back and straightened, his dark gaze meeting her huge, bewildered eyes with clinical detachment, and of all that was inexplicable about him she found his expression at that moment the most puzzling, and the most disturbing.

She felt his fingers trail lightly across the arc of her collarbone as his hand fell from her shoulder, and a convulsive shiver rippled down her spine. Then he smiled, and suddenly in his lean, handsome face was the calculating boardroom manipulator.

'I have a proposition for you,' said Harper briskly.

He was far too complex to understand, and too fascinating to turn away from. Nikki began to feel punch drunk. 'What kind of proposition?' she asked, eyeing him as warily as she might a hooded cobra.

Dark eyes lit with amusement, he drawled, 'Why, a business one, of course. I want to buy some artwork from you.'

Was that really all he wanted from her? She did not know what showed in her expression, but caution had her turning towards Peter's empty desk to hide it. 'If you want any of the advertising material you talked about earlier,' she said flatly, 'you'll have to discuss it with Peter.'

'Not applicable,' he stated with decisive, compelling authority. 'You see, the picture I want to buy from you is one you haven't painted yet.'

Her dark, bent head snapped up and around in astonishment, the blue eyes wearing a startled frown as she replied, 'But I don't do commissioned work. I—I don't know whether I'd be any good at it.'

The unpredictable slant of Harper's sleek brows became more pronounced. 'Then don't you think it's about time you tried?' he returned. 'All I want to do is reserve your next piece of work. You may paint whatever subject you like. The painting may be large or small; I don't care. The only stipulation I would put on you is that you spend not less than six months on it. I would, of course, adjust the price accordingly.'

He suggested a monetary figure that was staggeringly huge, but Nikki barely registered the amount. Staring, she exclaimed, 'Six months! I've never spent an entire six months on any single project before! How can you ask such a thing? How can you say beforehand how long a painting will take? That's absurd!'

'Not quite,' said Harper softly. His brown eyes pierced hers, the expression on his lean face turned into a forceful challenge. 'As I said before, when you've matured into your talent, you will be quite breathtaking, but there is not a single piece I have seen this morning that I would consider buying, because you have yet to explore how far you can push yourself. I don't want promise, I want fulfilment.'

'How dare you?' she expostulated, stiffening in outrage. Nobody had ever rejected her work like that before!

The smile that thinned his lips was almost contemptuous as he replied coolly, 'How do I dare speak to you in such a way, or how do I dare hold an independent opinion? The simple truth is, my girl, you do not live in a citadel, and I do not lower my standards for anyone.'

Nikki's nostrils flared as she sucked in a harsh breath, as stunned as if he had reached out with one of those gentle hands and slapped her. The ineffable composure with which he had replied yanked ruthlessly at her perspective. She felt at once very young and inexperienced, angry and hurt, and the boredom in Harper's face told her that he saw it and was totally unimpressed.

Certainly nobody had ever dismissed her work so cavalierly. She had studied in one of the world's most exclusive Parisian schools, and had received nothing but praise and encouragement from wholly dedicated, superb teachers. Even Peter was smug about his carefully orchestrated manipulation of her career. If she had a high opinion of her work, it was simply a reflection from everyone around her.

How arrogant she had become, Nikki realised, whitening still further. How arrogant, and how complacent. Harper was right; she had gone unchallenged for far too long, and she was absolutely furious at the insufferable manner he had used to make her see it.

And she also knew, in a flash of insight, that his was the unusually subtle mind that had matched the outstanding pieces of art in the lounge of his Mayfair house.

The knowledge of that forced her to choke back her fury and say, coldly, because she hated to admit it, 'You realise, of course, that the exercise could be a total disaster? I couldn't vouch for the quality of the painting, since I don't know what effect the time constraint would have on my technique.'

'I've considered the possibility,' replied Harper distantly, sweeping his gaze down the length of her body as if in reappraisal of her merits and potential weaknesses. The muscles in her jaw clenched under another wave of pure, unadulterated rage, for that single downward glance made her feel as if she was physically on an auction block and for sale to the highest bidder. 'But, from what I've seen today, I'm willing to take that chance. You would get paid for the painting, no matter what. But don't take too long to decide, will you? I won't wait long.'

God, but he was behaving in a detestable manner! She bit out acidly, 'You would have to wait six months, wouldn't you?'

'With the guarantee of an end result,' he pointed out, then added with sardonic amusement, 'no matter what it might be.'

That was the last straw. 'Right,' said Nikki with glittering eyes and a tight, furious smile, 'I'll take you up on your proposition but at my price, not yours.'

He had already offered her a king's ransom for a possible failure, and something flickered at the back of his dark gaze that might have been cynicism, or the beginnings of distaste as he drawled, 'I'm open to negotiation.'

'My own standards are far too high to accept payment for a potential failure,' she stated, bristling with a contempt of her own as she tilted her head to stare haughtily down her little nose at him. 'Although, to be sure, you must have too much money if you're willing to throw away so much on a gamble. No, my price is much more expensive than money. First, if I do your painting, you must give Peter the account you took so much trouble to discuss this morning.'

'Done,' he said immediately. 'If you're the designer who does the artwork. You'll have to complete that project before you start your commission, however, for it won't wait.'

'Fair enough,' she said with dangerous softness, 'but there's just one other condition. If I agree to this, you must sit for me, as many times as I need, and as often as I want. I have a fancy to do the portrait of the very rich and reclusive Harper Beaumont. It would make such an excellent exhibition piece and be so popular, don't you agree?'

She had managed to pierce through his formidable façade. Harper stiffened, his grey head rearing back, his face darkening into anger at her deliberate insolence. He snapped, 'That's quite unacceptable!'

'Isn't it just?' she agreed in a hard voice, which arrested his gaze. 'I never expected you to consent to it, Harper. I just wanted you to feel a little like you might be put up for sale, because it isn't at all pleasant, especially if you suspect you might be found somewhat lacking, and that is precisely how you've managed to make me feel today. I might be arrogant, and I might not be challenged enough, but I also have every bit as much pride as you do!'

A stark silence fell over the room as they glared at each other and then, amazingly, Harper began to laugh out loud. His entire handsome face was vivid with the overwhelming charm of it, prompting Nikki to stare unabashedly.

'What a surprise you are!' he exclaimed deeply. 'I thought to pique you into the challenge, but I obviously overshot the mark by a mile. I am sorry, Nikki. I should have broached the subject with more sensitivity.'

And how unlike him, considering his skill in dealing with Peter. What did that mean?

He was insufferable, overbearing, and too damned gracious. She looked away as she jerked one shoulder in unwilling acknowledgement of the apology, because she still wanted to be angry with him and was failing dismally. Clothing rustled, a tiny almost soundless warning that prickled along her skin, as he approached.

He put his hand underneath her chin and gently urged her to look at him. 'Shall we try again?' he murmured, still with that smile which was so impossible to deny. 'Nikki, I am visually jaded, and so bored that I can hardly remember why I first started buying art, but you have an exciting quality in your work that is as unpredictable as you are. Explore your world of potential. Challenge yourself like a new bird, and let me watch the first flight.'

'Flattery,' she muttered, a shaky defence against the inexorable tug in his chocolate-rich eyes. At that moment she looked very vulnerable and uncertain, and completely unaware of how trustingly her chin rested in the hollow of his curled fingers.

'Shall I try blackmail and bribery as well?' said Harper, his smile turning into a distinctly wicked grin. 'Your Peter won't get his account without it. And if you do agree, I'll sit for you, if you like. But you must give me first option to buy the portrait.'

'You'd be very good in the nude,' she murmured without thinking, and immediately her blue gaze turned stricken and she blushed a very deep red.

'Thank you,' he purred as he let his fingers slide an inch along her jawline. 'I'm so glad you think so. But that might call for even more—intense negotiation.'

'I—I didn't mean to suggest——' she stammered, appalled at the level of embarrassment she felt, at the crackle of electric sensation that shot from his warm hand down the length of her throat. 'That—that is—I wouldn't presume——'

He laughed gently, and before she could pull away bent to place a swift kiss beside her mouth, then let her go. Nikki didn't even have time to react. 'I know what you did. You were judging me with the eyes of an artist. It was a compliment. So, we're settled, then—one picture for me, one portrait for you, and one account for Peter. Now everybody's happy.'

'What?' she murmured, bemused by the speed with which he seemed to have tied her into the agreement.

Had she agreed? She must have, or at least he thought she had, but what exactly had she said? Thus ran her confused thinking, and the eminently skilled negotiator in front of her well knew it. He didn't give her a chance to recover, but went on smoothly, 'It leads me to one other point: you do realise that your present situation won't do?'

'What?' she said again, blankly. 'What present situation?'

Harper's eyebrows rose, and he looked rather surprised at her obtuseness. 'Why, the state of your hands, of course. A two-week delay on the marketing material I need is not acceptable, but I think I have a solution. You would need to do research on all the different aspects of my business before you can come up with some ideas of your own. You can be doing that while you convalesce, but do you honestly think those cuts will heal properly without giving them the rest they need? Gordon did warn you to keep as inactive as possible, but that's not going to happen while you stay on your own. Tell me, who did your hair and make-up today?'

Nikki almost told him. She hesitated, mouth open, but said nothing as her obstinate gaze wavered and fell. Harper's mouth compressed slightly as if he struggled to keep back a smile, and he went on briskly, 'Well, there you have it. You can't even wash your own hair properly without breaking your cuts open, let alone cook yourself decent meals. You'll just have to come home with me.'

By that time, Nikki reflected in the tiny corner of her reeling brain that was still capable of reflection, she was beginning to sound like a parrot as she practically shrieked, '*What*? But you can't be serious—I couldn't possibly——'

'I am serious, and you can possibly. In fact you will,' he stated, in the most reasonable tone of voice while wearing a most determined expression. Coupled with his forceful features, it had all the effect of a bulldozer. 'It's an excellent idea. I'll take you to my house in Oxfordshire. There's loads of room and the gardens are lovely. You'll enjoy it, and, what's more important, you'll be on hand to study everything of the business you need, and I can answer any questions you might have. That should cut down the delay as much as possible.'

'Oxfordshire?' she gabbled, so tied up in knots that she could barely peek out of herself, let alone make any sense. 'I thought you lived in London?'

'No, I stay the week in London, for business reasons, and the weekends in Oxford.' Harper did let himself smile then, at the hectic flush along her high cheekbones and the palpable distress she tried so hard to disguise. 'Things can get noisy in Oxford. You see, I have a six-year-old nephew in permanent residence, house staff tripping over themselves for something to do, and a mother who is a consistent Sunday visitor, aside from any possible weekend guests.'

'Oh, a mother,' said Nikki ridiculously. She was behaving like such a fool; for God's sake, why couldn't she pull herself together?

He gave her a very strange look. 'Gordon comes out now and then, as well. So, you see, you wouldn't lack for company; the staff can spoil you rotten, and your hands will heal much better. Oh, and if you're worried about any lack of privacy with all that lot, don't. There's a spare room over the garage, quite big, complete with hotplate and bathroom, if you need to get away from everyone. What more could you want?'

He was rushing her. Suddenly Nikki saw something else. For all his implication for an on-the-spot inspiration, he did not act as if he were surprised at his own proposal. He had come into Peter's office with every intention of making the offer.

The awareness calmed her obscurely. She replied steadily, 'I could ask you why. Why make such an offer to someone you didn't even know existed yesterday?'

The blue eyes studied him, troubled, so terribly wary, instinctively tending towards disbelief and cynicism, like a stray pup that was more used to a kick and a curse rather than a gentle touch and a kind word. If he said anything even remotely altruistic, she would brand him a liar, and nothing would convince her to change her mind.

A shadow like sadness flickered over the hard planes and angles of Harper's face before his expression hardened into a ruthless, predatory glitter, and, like a bloodthirsty child who saw villains where before she had only been suspicious, Nikki shrank back with an inaudible gasp. He—the epitome of the British gentleman, drawling, reserved, urbane, so sophisticated in dress and manner—suddenly seemed barely human. She looked at him and remembered the violence of his hold on her when she had run into him last night, and remembered, too, how she had compared him to a wolf.

'Let's just say I protect my investments,' he said low in his throat, like a growl.

Peter was no help whatsoever. Although he was only behaving in a predictable manner as they sat in his office after Harper had left, Nikki chose to see his attitude as a personal betrayal, for it gave her a chance to vent a confused spate of bitter feeling. She curled up in the chair in front of his desk, wincing as her wounded palms throbbed.

'You just have to go; you have to,' Peter said emphatically. 'He made it clear that it's the one way we can keep his account, and in fact I'm only grateful he's willing to wait for your hands to heal—for a little while there I was afraid we'd lost him.'

'I look to you for some moral support, and this is what I get!' she grumbled, grudgingly accepting the glass of Perrier he poured for her.

'No,' contradicted Peter drily, 'you're looking to me to echo all your doubts and fears about this invitation from Harper Beaumont. Well, I won't! It's the most reasonable suggestion he could have made so you can start on the work as soon as possible. I confess, I envy you like mad. I'd give my eye-teeth for an invitation from him—most people would, and all you can do is complain about it! Honestly, I don't know what you're so worked up about. Aside from the sound business sense, it was a very considerate offer. Besides, even if you're intimidated by him, didn't he say he was hardly ever home?'

'Yes,' she muttered reluctantly, feeling even more disgruntled than ever. She needed to set up all those doubts and fears: they were barriers against Harper and his invitation, for the man set off such a riotous confusion in her head that she didn't know which way to turn. Her alarm bells were clanging deafeningly, setting off every instinct to dive for the nearest cover. But just as strong an impulse in the other direction was the urge to take him up on his offer, just for any chance she could get to satisfy this compulsive fascination he held for her.

For the last ten years of her life Nikki had been content enough to label men as very odd creatures indeed, a

Pandora's box she had no intention of ever opening. Young men her own age were insipid by comparison to the level of sophistication she had grown up with.

Her father had embodied the same powerful charisma that Harper had, and anyone who lived within the magic golden circle of his influence resided in Camelot until he had died and the enchanted air she had inhabited for the first twelve years of her life disintegrated.

Her mother had grown addicted to powerful men and soon remarried, and her stepfather, too, had something of the magnetic touch, but something in Nikki rebelled at being sucked into the vortex of another person's life. Her independence meant too much to her; she worked too hard to maintain it, and gained too much pleasure out of carving her livelihood for herself.

What Harper awakened in her, she realised suddenly, was a deep distrust of herself. For every decent characteristic he showed, for every human foible, every rare gentleness, every apology, she gravitated towards him, understanding, sympathising, feeling a deep affinity for the part of himself he held in reserve from the rest of the world.

But then a glimpse of his hard ruthlessness appeared, an iron hand in a velvet glove, and Nikki kicked up her heels to run away in a panic. But nothing happened. He didn't threaten her; she cried wolf and the wolf wasn't there.

So which of her reactions should she operate on? Neither seemed appropriate, but she couldn't let go of them both, even if Harper said he wouldn't be at his Oxford home except for the weekends. For instance, just what was she supposed to feel now—disappointed at the prospect of his long absences, or relieved? And why couldn't she shake off the imperative hold his invitation had on her?

Part of her was angry as well, at how he had manoeuvred her into this extremely uncomfortable position. She was caught between a rock and a hard place; if she rejected his offer, then he would withdraw his account from Peter's business, and she would have to contend with the inevitable strain that put on Peter's and her relationship, especially as she couldn't seem to offer any sound reason for the rejection. But if she accepted—well, that meant she would have to contend with Harper and all his disturbing nuances, even down to the inexplicable kiss that had taken place right in this very office.

'So have you decided what you're going to do?' asked Peter anxiously, watching her expressive, pointed face as her silence stretched for too long.

'I don't have to decide until noon tomorrow,' muttered Nikki as she shook her dark head in disgust. 'That's when he's dropping by on his way out to Oxford, to see if I've made up my mind.'

That was not the strict truth. Harper had said, just before stalking out of the door, that he was on his way out to Oxford tomorrow and would pick her up at noon, so be packed and ready. But the bristling, independent side to Nikki's personality absolutely refused to acknowledge it as an order. At best he had simply assumed she would come, which was quite arrogant enough, and if she decided she wouldn't go she just wouldn't answer her front door.

How rude of her. She couldn't contemplate doing that, not while looking into Peter's hopeful gaze. Oh, dear, why did Harper have to put her in such a quandary?

Peter was saying, 'If you do decide to go, you will give me a ring and let me know where I can contact you?'

'Of course,' she said.

'That's it, then. What a wonderful coup we've managed today; I just know you'll do the right thing.'

She sighed heavily. 'Look, I'd better go. I've a million and one things to do. And I am sorry about not being able to finish the other projects.'

'Not to worry, love,' Peter said, then added slyly, 'If you managed to procure Harper's account, it more than makes up for everything.'

Unfair, unfair, she said, but silently and without heat, for she wasn't sure whether she meant Harper, Peter or herself.

The day had worn on for too long; by the time she made her way home the Friday afternoon rush-hour had started and it seemed to take forever before she was letting herself into her small flat.

She got a Chinese take-away and ate it ravenously, for she had missed lunch. Afterwards she washed the make-up off her face and cried weary tears as soapy water slid underneath the plastic bags she'd fastened at her wrists. It soaked into the bandages, stinging her cuts as painfully as if she'd sprinkled salt on to them.

She had to strip off the wet dressings, an awkward and even more painful business, and as she had nothing else to use she re-dressed her hands with clean strips of linen.

The next few weeks began to seem like an endless expanse of time, made dreary by a succession of small tasks which had, as a result of her injury, become tedious and drawn-out. House staff tripping over themselves for want of things to do? she thought sourly, yanking a long

T-shirt on and crawling into bed. Well. She could allow them to look after her—just for a few weeks. Just until her hands were better. And she'd be doing Peter a favour.

She could handle Harper, if she had to. Hadn't she done so today? If he had manipulated her, she had done just as much to him, and could count it a triumph that she could procure on her own, albeit on Harper's terms, such a valuable account for Peter's company. Not only that, but she had negotiated for his portrait as well. They had each given in a little to get what they wanted.

Besides, she wanted to know if Harper could be trusted—that quiet, wise man with the gentle hands who guarded himself behind those hard, watchful eyes. She wanted to find out if there was any decent substance behind the arrogance of the man who was bred to power. That was the simplest, deepest truth.

The night's rest did her good. Nikki was packed, and her suitcase waiting by the door when she went to the local tea shop for a leisurely breakfast of croissants with butter and strawberry jam, reading a weekend paper over several cups of coffee. Then she nipped into the nearest chemist for some cotton pads and gauze, and the pharmacist on duty was perfectly willing to help her clean and dress her wounds properly. She spent more time talking with the pharmacist than she had really meant to, so when she finally strolled back to her flat it was almost eleven-thirty.

Though the English weather in May was still gusty and had not settled into a summertime pattern, her neighbourhood was in glorious bloom with daffodils, blossoming cherry trees and the first of the year's rose-buds.

Nikki was so busy admiring the lovingly tended, tiny city gardens that she almost didn't notice the black

Jaguar parked at the end of the little mews, and she certainly didn't register the implications until she saw the tall grey-haired man who strolled towards her.

Stupid surprise rattled crazily through her as she looked up into Harper's quiet, smiling gaze—stupid because she had known he would be along any time now, surprise because he was dressed so casually in jeans and a Shetland sweater. He seemed like another person altogether. This was an entirely more comfortable, approachable man, outside of the environment she had mentally placed him in and yet in his element.

'Oh, hello,' she said as she stared at him. 'I didn't expect you so soon.'

The truth was, she didn't expect this at all, and her image of him took a tiny, irrevocable shift. He reached for the plastic bag she carried that was full of her various purchases from the morning and she relinquished it automatically, as he said, 'I thought I'd drop by a little early to see if you needed help with anything like taking out your rubbish.'

A smile broke over her face. 'Thank you,' she replied. 'I was about to take out all the perishables from my refrigerator and do just that. I'm all packed, though.'

Harper shortened his long, characteristically impatient stride and fell into step beside her, so tall in comparison with her slight figure, so lean yet muscled with an innate athletic power which gave his broad shoulders an aggressive depth. 'Good,' he said deeply, sounding amused. 'I'd half expected you to back out.'

'I was half inclined to do so,' she confessed, fitting her key with some effort into the door. He reached out and forestalled her by putting his hands over hers and holding her still, so that her blue gaze flew to his in sharp, slightly anxious enquiry.

'Nikki, have I ever given you reason to be afraid of me?' he asked, but in such a way that all possible threat was taken out of the question.

How strong he was, and how reliant one could become on the care with which he cloaked it. His brown eyes were vivid with the expression he would not allow his expression to reveal. They were eyes to drown oneself in, deep, searching pools that took every bit as much as they gave, multiplying the intensity of feeling inside her so that she sighed, at once a release and an admission.

'It's not fear, at least not precisely,' she said, her lips softened and vulnerable on the words that were quiet, yet steady. 'I never did object to your invitation in itself, but I do have doubts as to how you made it. I am very wary of men who know how to manipulate as well as you do, and that's a hard habit to break. I'm not even sure whether it's a habit that should be broken.'

He frowned and seemed about to say something, but then just shrugged, and smiled, and carried her bandaged hand up to press a light kiss on the small fingers that smelled faintly of antiseptic. Then, as always, he released her almost immediately so that she had no opportunity to withdraw. He turned the key in the lock for her and commented, 'You look better. Still a little pale, though. Did you have a busy day yesterday?'

The adroit change in conversation gave her a handle on recovering her poise, and she laughed, expostulating, 'Very, and who do I have to thank for that?'

'Your Peter is a rather excitable man,' said Harper smoothly.

'I think his wife would object to your calling him "my Peter",' she retorted very drily as he stood back and let her precede him up the stairs. A ghost of a quiet laugh wafted up from behind her and enveloped her in velvet auditory sensation, calling forth an answering, irrepressible grin. She smothered it quickly as she came up to the third-floor landing, blaming her breathlessness on the swift ascent while Harper showed no such physical weakness. She had to grope for some lingering sense of outrage to add acidic sarcasm to her next comment. 'And yes, he is, but then one would expect him to be after how you enticed him yesterday. He feels much indebted to your business contribution, of course.'

'How rude you are when you're being sardonic,' returned Harper, effectively taking the wind out of her sails by jangling the forgotten keys in front of her nose. 'Which one will let us into your eyrie?'

The pertly upturned nose just two inches from his fingers wrinkled in a very haughty sniff. She indicated, and he unlocked again, and as she led him into her flat she felt a wild sense of suffocation at how the spacious room contracted almost violently with the onslaught of his dynamic presence.

Nikki stood to one side as he prowled through the place in just a few of those distance-dominating strides. He flicked a keen glance around, noting the untidy jumble of books, the attractive hide-a-bed couch, the contradicting neatness of her art supplies in the middle of the hardwood floor, the soft canvas suitcase ready by the door.

She hadn't realised it before, but the flat was a very private cocoon where few people were allowed to intrude. She saw it suddenly though his eyes and felt somehow exposed, like a nocturnal animal blinking in full sunlight, and for some reason she couldn't bear to hear him make some personal comment on the place.

He didn't, merely sending her a quick, brisk smile as he said, 'I'll rifle through your refrigerator for you. Want everything out?'

'Yes, please.' Nikki hovered as he dispensed efficiently with the few perishables in the waist-high unit, jumping forward to take the open carton of milk out of his hands and dump the liquid down the sink.

'Have you had breakfast?' he asked, straightening with the rubbish bag slung in one hand. 'If not, we can stop along the way for something to eat.'

'I've already eaten, thank you.' She frowned as she turned the tap to run cold water into the sink and rinse away the last traces of milk, and she couldn't have explained the frown to save her life.

Except, perhaps, that Harper seemed to have taken her over since he had first appeared, and that had never happened to her before. She felt distinctly uncomfortable, as if she had given away part of the independence that was so precious to her, and it was no good trying to rationalise about how much control she had theoretically over events; he had invaded her mind and dominated her thinking, and no one could do that without at least some partial co-operation.

'I see you've also had your hands re-bandaged,' he observed from too close by her shoulder. She snapped the water flow off with a sharp flick of the wrist, ignoring the warning twinge from the palm of her hand at the hasty gesture, and schooled her expression to unrevealing blandness as she turned back to face him.

They left the flat together and Nikki waited for Harper to return from the rubbish tip, her suitcase on the ground beside her. Though she had never taken off the light denim jacket she had worn to the shops that morning, the wind sliced through both it and her sweater, and she hunched herself into a shivering huddle.

Those dark, keen eyes saw too much, and all she had as some kind of potential defence was instinct. She would have to hide very carefully the strange, premonitory feelings that had shuttled through her like a fast midnight train, that had her wondering why her life seemed to be taking on a whole new sense of direction.

She was only going to Oxford for a week or two. She refused even to consider why it felt as if she was going on a journey from which she would never return, for he would see it in her face. She didn't even dare acknowledge to herself why it was so important he did not.

He returned and asked, as his gaze pierced into hers and seemed to read all of her secrets, 'Are you ready?'

'As ready as I'll ever be,' she muttered as she ducked her head, but she hadn't meant to make her reply sound quite so grim.

CHAPTER FOUR

NIKKI compressed her mouth into a tight line as she settled into the passenger-seat of the Jaguar and Harper reached across to pull over her seatbelt and buckle it. It was hard to avoid his observant gaze in the confines of the car, especially when he was twisted neatly around at his taut, lean waist, the broad, rolling shoulders angled towards her, one long arm resting for a moment on the steering-wheel in unavoidable confrontation.

He was too much to take at close quarters. She jerked her head towards her window and pretended to stare out of it, while she listened to her idiotic heart thumping in mad concert with her chaotic thoughts. Too much, too large, too sure of himself with a kind of unaffected panache that came with experience and maturity, too male.

And, of course, too accurate, as he settled back in his own seat and started the car, remarking quietly, 'I know how uncomfortable you must find the restrictions at the moment.'

She ground out a blushing admission of her intense frustration. 'I just hate feeling so helpless. It hurts even to make myself a cup of tea!'

'I'm not surprised,' he replied with studied casualness. 'Your poor hands took a good slashing. But you aren't helpless, you're just slightly incapacitated for the time being, and I think you're being very commonsensical about accepting some assistance. Have patience, it won't last long.'

Harper sped the Jaguar around Hyde Park and past Marble Arch. He coped with the Saturday traffic in London just as he coped with everything else—with a spare economy of effort that was highly efficient without being ostentatious. He was never flashy or boastful of his own capabilities; he simply got the job done with a minimum of fuss. Somewhat surprisingly, Nikki was not daunted by this aspect of his considerably forceful personality. Instead she found it soothing, rock-steady and weatherproof, something to be relied upon in a very unstable world.

She said after a few minutes, with a slight smile, 'You always seem to know the right thing to say.'

That prompted a very satirical glance from under raised eyebrows. He said drily, 'Do I? I don't remember doing so well at it yesterday.'

'Granted, you didn't hit it perfectly,' returned Nikki, her smile turning somewhat sour. 'You certainly ruffled my feathers when you rubbed me the wrong way. But didn't you get what you wanted in the end?'

'Yes, I got what I wanted,' Harper replied thoughtfully. 'But in marketing terms for my company, and you're taking on the challenge of a new painting that I have high hopes for. Because you're so much of a perfectionist, I can afford to admit to the high hopes without fearing that I'm putting undue pressure on you. But, as you pointed out earlier, does that justify the methods I used?'

So he had taken in what she had said, and not just ignored it. Nikki remained silent, which was an answer all of its own. They had reached the western arc of the North Circular Road, where the traffic was moving at a snail's pace. Harper slowed the car without the slightest hint of impatience, as if he had all the time in the world for this shared journey, and he flicked a quick glance at her, smiling at her troubled expression.

'I shall confess something to you,' he said lightly, as if to indicate that what he next said was amusing, of no import. 'You're good for me. You have a very strong personality that is a challenge in itself, and those un-relentingly perceptive blue eyes of yours make me see how I have slid into a kind of behaviour that ten years ago I would have considered unacceptable. My career is concerned with results, not the morality of the method, and there is nothing at present in my personal life to curb my particular brand of arrogance.'

'I guess I'm not surprised,' she said after a moment. 'If Peter, and Duncan Chang, and Gordon, and the police are any kind of example of what you face, you must get very tired of being thrust into a demi-god status.'

'You sound as if you've had first-hand experience of that sort of thing,' remarked Harper with frown.

'I've certainly lived with and around enough powerful men to believe I understand it,' she replied, staring at the brooding expression that had settled over his face. He did not like what he was hearing, but at least he was receptive to it. 'You have to be hard, because you make so many hard decisions that you've got to live with. You've got to be ruthless, because the people around you are ruthless. And when that spills into your personal life people around you start to look at you with more awe than respect and the distance widens between you and the rest of the world. In a lot of men that brings out all the darker side of their personalities. Solitary confinement can create quite an imbalance.'

'I could almost wish you didn't see me quite so well.' He said it softly, the hard white teeth gleaming at the utterance, but Nikki saw how his beautifully formed fingers gripped the steering-wheel.

Well, exposure was sometimes painful. Her own hand went out of its own volition and rested on the rigid length of his muscled thigh. 'Shall I confess something to you now?' she said, and as he heard the unsteadiness in her voice his left hand came down to curl around her wrist. 'Sometimes I am afraid around you. The reason isn't who you are or what you've done. I like and respect what I see in you. But you resurrect some memories that are difficult for me. I'm frightened of them, Harper. Not of you.'

He sent her a quick, astute glance while his clasp tightened. 'Was it your father?'

'Oh, in part,' she said wearily, making a small, inadequate gesture with her free hand.

He was listening intently, and when she didn't continue he prompted, 'He died when you were about eleven, or twelve, didn't he?'

She gasped in shock, then exclaimed, 'How long have you known?'

He shrugged. 'I guessed somewhere between yesterday afternoon and this morning. I'm not sure when—perhaps a trick of movement on your part, or a turn of phrase. Your name was another clue, of course. Nikki Ashton—Nicholas Ashton-Meyer. Did you drop the Meyer for professional reasons?'

'Yes, I didn't want anyone to be influenced because of who I was.' She became aware of the tremor running through her body; he must be able to feel it, and she made an effort to withdraw.

He wouldn't let her. 'I saw your father at university once, when he visited for a guest lecture. He was a very charismatic man, but then he wouldn't have become such a prominent politician if he hadn't been.'

'We were all under the influence of his aura. It was a fairy-tale life, in many ways,' she sighed, as she leaned her head back, shaken by the intensity of her reaction to Harper's shrewd guess.

'Tell me, Nikki?'

He asked gently. He asked as if it really mattered. And it suddenly did; her long silence was no longer self-protective but burdensome.

'We went everywhere with him,' she said quietly and closed her eyes to see it all again, the brilliant parade of different places. 'An entire entourage of family, private tutors, secretaries and advisers. Hong King, China for a year, here in England, Saudi Arabia, when he was involved in negotiating that old deal in the seventies, France for the nuclear disarmament talks.'

'I remember,' he murmured, an unobtrusive encouragement.

The scenery alongside the M40 flashed by, beautifully rolling hills and picturesque villages bathed in golden sunshine. Nikki didn't see a thing. 'When Senator Ashton-Meyer spoke,' she said drily, 'people jumped. It was no secret that he was a brilliant candidate for the presidency. We were all caught up in the golden reflection. My brother Johnny and I idolised him. I wonder if he knew just how much we heard, of speculations and power manoeuvres, political decisions based on the bottom line of expediency. He could annihilate a character with such witty charm. My mother was totally immersed in his life. It crippled her when he was killed.'

'How did it affect you and your brother?'

'Oh, astonishment, numb disbelief. We were too young to discover any feet of clay to our idol, you see, and didn't recognise until we were much older how narcissistic he was, and how dependent he was on the adulation of everyone around him. Don't get me wrong; he wasn't a bad man, just selfish. It was hard to conceive that someone so invincible could die. All the magical impetus that put the sparkle in our lives was just—gone. Mother was like a ghost for nearly a year.'

'Then she remarried right about that time, didn't she? To Karle Heissenger, the rich German art collector?'

'Yes,' Nikki said, her voice very wry. 'Then she married Karle.'

Harper's expression was neutral as he asked, 'So you and Heissenger don't get along?'

Her resultant smile was tight; how many times had she already seen how astute he was? He noticed every slip, every crack in the façade. 'Quite the contrary,' she said ironically. 'My relationship with Karle is extremely polite.'

She felt rather than saw the keen stab of his enquiring glance. 'Then what did he do to alienate you?'

Nikki smiled and lifted her shoulders. 'Absolutely nothing. Karle is simply as my father was—seduced by his own glamour and not particularly interested in another man's children, except for the possible value they might have as adornments to his lifestyle. By that point in my life I was more than happy to go to boarding-school in Paris, and return to the States for holidays and Christmases. Home just didn't feel like home any more. At least not the kind I was used to.'

'And you stayed to carve a life of your own.'

'And I stayed,' she agreed. 'You see, reflected glory has such a limited appeal. What kind of real success would I have were I to rely on my stepfather's influence? What kind of independence? Neither he, nor my mother, really understands. They view my insistence on living within my earning power as an amusing personality quirk, and are just waiting for the day when I tire of my working-girl status and return to débutante balls and discreet flirtations with elegant young men from very acceptable families. How very eccentric of me not to concede.'

Harper grinned, a blade-slash of wicked amusement. 'Indeed,' he murmured drily, almost to himself, 'and the last piece in the puzzle.'

'What do you mean?'

The firm hold he had on her was at once an anchor and a lure, for suddenly she surfaced from that backward dive of reminiscence into the present. Again she tried to tug her arm away, a small and furtive effort to reclaim her own space; in response Harper rubbed the ball of his thumb along the sensitive skin of her inner wrist, producing a convulsive shiver down the back of her spine.

'Only that I can now see the reasons why you're so prickly about your independence,' he replied after a moment. 'For you it isn't a given—you've had to fight for it every step of the way.'

'Oh, it's not so bad,' she said, her light shrug a disguise for the shrewd glance she sent him. 'Their motives might be misguided, but their intentions are good, I think. I just happen to believe that expediency is not the bottom line, the easy road isn't always the best one, and I know how much self-respect can get lost when you're involved with powerful people. I won't pay that price again, because the morality of the method always matters, Harper. It always matters.'

No matter how quietly it was said, the warning was crystal-clear, and it shot home. She peeked quickly at

Harper to find him in a frozen state that had nothing to do with driving along an even, straight road. Then came the thaw, and vivid reaction, and he said, sounding queerly rueful, 'Sharp as a tack and ruthlessly honest to the death. My dear girl, I don't misuse the influence I have. I'm a protector, not a destroyer.'

'Yes?' she murmured almost dreamily as she stared at him, half in inexplicable longing, half in trepidation. 'But what about your enemies? What about the people in your life who dare to say no?'

Deafening silence greeted that, and if he had seemed frozen before, now the tough line of his profile was encased in ice. 'If you think to set yourself up as some kind of judge over my behaviour,' he bit out acidly, 'I advise you to stop right where you are. I give no accounts for what I do, and you are not my keeper.'

A dark simmer of explosive emotion roiled inside her as he threw a quick glare at her, and Nikki sat back in her seat, at once intimidated and fascinated by the eruptive anger she had provoked. 'My father never could stand to be crossed or questioned either,' she breathed, unable to help herself, and if anything his anger intensified.

'Stop trying to compare me to the men you've known, and start coming to your own conclusions! I am not your father!' he snapped. 'And if all you're looking for is a replacement for him, you can forget it!'

That came as an unexpected slap; she hated how he had seen through her wariness to the self-doubt her pride had not let her fully acknowledge. Nikki exclaimed violently, 'Looking for a replacement! God forbid! If anything, my father taught me what to be wary of, and what to avoid in a man! I'm not looking for anything—I'm quite content with my life just the way it is, thank you!'

'Content?' he replied sharply. 'Oh, yes, I can see how you would be content in your tidy little life, unchallenged, unprovoked, untouched. How safely you have everything arranged for yourself, and what a pity that real life doesn't conform to the neat pigeon-holes you've laid out!'

Incredulous anger seared her words with a harsh bite as Nikki snapped, 'How do you know what my life is like? You know some of my past, not all of it. You think you understand me. Well, you don't. Not yet; not at all!'

'You think I don't know you?' he returned, with a softness far more dangerous than his explosive anger. 'Or that I can't see the deeper reasons for what you do? You think I didn't feel your withdrawal when I kissed you yesterday, or that I don't know what you were really warning me about when you told me of Heissenger and your father, and why you keep trying to compare me to either man? That is a convenient illusion, but not one you can hide behind.'

A thousand-watt lightbulb flashed in her head. She could certainly take her own sweet time about it, but if she was smacked in the face hard enough with a fact eventually it got past the thick skull and sank in.

Well, of course. He was as attracted to her as she was to him, but because of his greater experience he'd seen it far before she ever came to the slow realisation. A swift-paced mental flashback reawakened the memory of the knowledgeable amusement in his eyes that very first night they'd met—of how she had kissed him on the cheek, and he had kissed her on the mouth.

From that moment on her memory shot ahead like a film fast-forwarded to the delicate dance he had con-. ducted in Peter's office yesterday, reading her reactions better than she read them herself, advancing inch by inch and retreating instantly at the first sign of a freeze-out.

This was a depth of truth she had never before experienced, nor knew how to deal with, and how did she feel? Miserable, confused, reeling inside with the shock of confrontation, and unable to think clearly about what the future held in store for her. The midnight train was still journeying towards an unknown, unseen horizon. Nikki was the midnight train, hurtling even faster along an unbeaten track, and she didn't know where she would stop or how, for Harper was the driver.

Instead of retreat or denial, she again took refuge in attack. 'Far be it from me to contradict you, since you seem to know all the answers!' she snapped. 'After all, you'll only believe what you wish to!'

And suddenly his own anger seemed gone, as completely as if it had never been. He replied coolly, with a deep frown, 'Is that how you see me? No, Nikki. I don't believe what I wish to. I believe what I am shown. You need have no worries while you stay at my house— nothing is going to happen between us that you don't want.'

That was when he made another rare mistake. It was entirely the wrong time to adopt such a patient, paternalistic attitude, and absolutely the wrong thing to say.

He acted so bland, she thought bitterly, so unaffected, so very much in control. A man with his universe made to order, and some men got too used to giving orders. How could he know what she did and didn't want? He would assume command of the situation, with that arrogant presumption he had for believing he always knew best, and with a sudden intensity that rippled through her like wildfire she hated the indomitable quality of that control and knew a dark, passionate desire to rip it to shreds.

The midnight train picked up speed. She could almost hear the wind shriek.

'Darling,' she drawled, her white heat evolving into a pointed sardonicism, '*I* could have told you that.'

He sucked in a harsh breath, a small, tell-tale reaction. Then he smiled a tiny violent smile that shook the earth, and she felt as if the driver of the midnight train had just taken his hand off the brake.

Harper's home in the outskirts of Oxford was a veritable mansion, but Nikki had already seen enough of his lifestyle to be prepared. After parking, he dragged out her suitcase while she climbed out of the car on legs made numb by the cataclysmic ride and stared in bemused pleasure at the sprawling Victorian house. It was everything she would have guessed from his eclectic personality: well maintained and gracious, nestling in a fenced six-acre plot like a jewel in an ornate setting of luscious colour. The front landscape was superb, and she knew the back garden would be just as impressive.

The front oak door was curiously enough the most battered part of the outside appearance, and the explanation was soon made self-evident as it crashed open on well-oiled hinges.

As the man beside her made some kind of exasperated murmur, out hurtled a small cannon-ball that crashed straight into Harper's legs with no discernible slackening of speed. Nikki winced. The cannon-ball resolved itself into a human boy with dark hair flopping into very dark brown eyes, already possessed of a hectic grace that would, with maturity, develop into a devastating pantherish stride.

'Hello, sport,' said Harper as he reached out with easy affection and ruffled the boy's head. As she watched, assembling first impressions with lightning speed, she could see the family resemblance, which was quite unmistakable. 'Been misbehaving as usual?'

His nephew chose to ignore that, and instead demanded, 'What *took* you so long?'

'I told you on the phone last night, remember?' replied Harper with no sign of impatience. Presumably, Nikki thought drily, his impatience was reserved for recalcitrant adults. 'I had to pick up a friend of mine who's going to be staying here for a while. Nikki, meet Charles.'

'Hi,' she said, as the boy's eyes turned to fix her with a gaze unsettlingly like his uncle's, direct and piercing.

'Hi,' he said, summing her up with that one glance. 'What happened to your hands?'

'I hurt them,' she said simply, with a quick look at Harper, who nodded in approval.

'I can see that!' he retorted, to which she muffled a laugh. 'I meant how did you hurt them?'

'Manners,' Harper warned with a stern weariness that did not cloak the affectionate indulgence beneath it. 'Charles, tell Anne we've arrived and ask her to scrounge up some coffee, will you? We'll take it in the rear lounge.'

'OK.' The boy turned to go, then sent her another dark look from under frowning brows. 'My name's Charles,' he advised her. 'Not Chuck, not Charlie, not Chas. Just Charles.'

Considerably startled, and struggling now to hide her laughter, Nikki managed to promise with due gravity, 'I'll remember.'

'Good,' he said with immense satisfaction, then turned to race back into the house in the same headlong, reckless fashion he had exited in.

Harper raised his voice in a deep shout, the unexpectedness of which made her jump. 'And mind the——'

The door slammed with such force that she could have sworn the sturdy oak trembled, and both of them winced that time. After the boy had disappeared, Harper shook his head in smiling resignation and set an easier pace towards the house. He asked, as Nikki fell into step beside him, 'Well, what do you think of him?'

The charged atmosphere that had built up in the car had quite dissipated upon their arrival. She felt as if she wanted to be disappointed, but was too shaken to feel anything but relief. With a slight grin, she replied, 'He's not exactly "mad, bad and dangerous to know" yet, but just give him another ten years and I think he'll manage it.'

'No truer word has been spoken in jest,' he said ruefully, even as his face softened. 'Think you can put up with him while you're here?'

'I think he's delightful,' she said in all honesty. 'How did he come to be living with you?'

'My sister Grace died shortly after he was born six years ago, and Charles's father was a Middle-East correspondent who was killed shortly after that, so I've more or less adopted him. Best thing for all concerned, really. Between them, my mother and Anne, my housekeeper, keep an eye on him through the week while I'm in London, but he's got more than enough space to spread without driving any one of us too crazy.'

He spoke in such a casual, offhand manner, simply explaining the facts of his lifestyle, but Nikki turned and stared at him as if she'd never seen him before. It must have been an extremely difficult time for all of them, especially for Harper, who had assumed guardianship of a tiny baby.

They must be more like father and son than uncle and nephew, and the image of him gently holding a small infant close to his breast was so evocative, so unexpectedly moving that she felt her throat go dry. Ah, but he would be a splendid father, stern and steady and eternally loving. Harper was the kind of man dynasties sprang from.

He led her without fuss through the massive front hall and directly up the front staircase. Nikki's mind whirled with the rich varied décor that was a perfect blend of traditional and modern, even down to the well-polished wooden floors upon which were thrown rugs containing a light pastel design. Harper was a living ghost throughout the entire house that reflected his tastes and personality.

'I'll put you in one of the back bedrooms,' he said over one broad shoulder, 'and you can see how you like it. You can move later if you'd prefer to go out to the flat over the garage, but for now it might be easiest to be under the same roof where the meals are cooked.'

'That sounds wonderful,' she murmured as she trailed behind him. The upstairs seemed to be a rabbit-warren that branched off the main landing, the halls she glimpsed small and therefore by necessity completely devoid of any furnishing except for the pictures hung on the walls at tasteful intervals. Her head craned back and forth greedily as she walked past a fortune in priceless art. 'How many bedrooms do you have?'

'Seven and a half,' he told her and she chuckled.

'How can you have half a bedroom?'

'There's a very small room that was originally intended as a nursery. It's right by Charles's, and he

claimed it last year for his toys.' He stopped at the door
at the end of the hall, which had taken a left turn, and
he sent her a slight smile. 'I've put you on the other side
of the house from him, but he has no sense of social
courtesy and will probably sniff you out at the soonest
opportunity.'

'I stand warned.' Then he threw open the door and
she gasped with delight. The bedroom he had chosen for
her was most charmingly decorated in an adaptation of
the traditional Victorian style and completely feminine
without being frilly, wallpapered with a pattern of tiny
rose-buds that complemented a marble-topped rosewood
vanity table. The wardrobe was gleaming mahogany, a
piece of art in itself, but what captured her affection was
the canopied four-poster bed piled high with embroidered pillows. There was a small fireplace opposite
it, and across from where she stood were French doors
that led out to a balcony.

'Do you like it?' he asked, smiling now with pleasure
as he watched her expressive face.

'Harper, it's beautiful. I love it.'

'Good.' He pointed to a small door close to one side
of the fireplace. 'You've a water closet over there, but
don't worry. It's fully modernised, and there's a shower
and bath installed. If you'd like to leave your things for
now, Anne will be up to unpack while we have coffee
and something to eat.'

She wanted to explore her bedroom and run out on
to the balcony to look around, but reluctantly she post-
poned the urge. 'That sounds wonderful.'

'What delightful manners you have. I suppose it's too
much to hope for that some of it will rub off on to
Charles,' Harper remarked with an ironic quirk of his

eyebrows. 'Speaking of which, he ought to come hunting for us any moment now.'

And, naturally, he was entirely correct. At the top of the staircase they collided with the boy, who scowled in perfectly believable surprise. Before she could help it, Nikki's infectious, irreverent laugh bubbled out. Charles's face assumed a carbon copy of Harper's own haughty arrogance, at which she laughed even harder, and then the boy's façade cracked and he grinned at her with an irrepressible charm that was all his own.

From that moment on, Charles was Nikki's voluble shadow throughout the afternoon. Harper settled himself in the rear lounge, a quiet, unobtrusive presence that flicked through the pile of his personal post which had collected through the week, while Nikki was dragged over every inch of the downstairs, from the kitchen to the library, and even all over the carefully plotted expanse of the back garden.

She met the housekeeper Anne, a greying woman in her fifties whose brisk, no-nonsense attitude concealed a heart of gold, and Anne's laconic Welsh husband Gavin, whose weather-beaten face lit up when she praised the grounds which were his pride and joy. They lived in a two-bedroom, self-contained basement flat that had been converted from an original storage cellar, accessible by a panelled door propped open in the kitchen.

Anne snapped indiscriminately at both Charles and the writhing chaos of three cats and two straggly scraps of dogs that resided in the warm, airy kitchen, then turned to say with a robust laugh to Nikki, 'They have this entire huge house and six acres to lose themselves in, and where do they congregate? Right under my feet!'

'One word from you and they do as they like!' agreed Nikki, blue eyes sparkling at the housekeeper. Charles did not deign to respond. He was sprawled most inconveniently in the middle of the kitchen floor, the sturdy length of his thin body folded on to itself as he reverted from his unsettling precociousness into frankly childish behaviour.

He was playing with one of the dogs, a floppy little nothing of a thing with anxious, eager eyes and a frantic tail. Nikki noticed the gentleness in the boy's small hands as he murmured to the animal, and her heart melted. The Beaumont males certainly knew how to crawl right past her inherent reserve, in one way or another, and they didn't even have to work at it. All they had to do was be themselves.

Supper was a simple affair of cold meats and salad, served with an excellent Moselle wine. Charles was allowed to stay up past his normal bedtime, and the boy grew very merry, until at last Harper hustled him upstairs for a bath and story-time.

Left to her own devices, Nikki wandered upstairs as well to the privacy of her bedroom, and spent some time in pleasurable exploration of its charms. Anne had been up some time earlier, and she found that all her things had been unpacked and neatly put away in the wardrobe and dresser, while her cosmetics and hairbrush were arranged on the rosewood vanity table.

She had just decided to take a shower and had stripped off her sweater when a quick knock sounded at her door, and she turned in the middle of the room, calling out, 'Come in.'

Harper poked his head around the corner, a startling intrusion into the intimacy of the surroundings. But his smile was cool and uncomplicated as he asked, 'Are you retiring for the evening, or would you like to come back downstairs?'

Nikki checked her watch. It had just gone nine o'clock, and she replied, 'I'm not ready for bed yet. I just want to have a shower first, and then I'll be down again shortly.'

His dark eyes studied her rather clinically. 'Can you manage all right with your hands? If you want help with washing your hair, all you have to do is say so.'

She flushed; she could feel it as a creeping warmth rising over her face and was extremely annoyed with herself for the reaction. 'I—are you sure you wouldn't mind?' she stammered, then went an even deeper colour. Perhaps she had misunderstood, and he had meant to send up Anne.

His smile had deepened with subtle amusement at the furiously dark colour staining her cheekbones, and he pushed her door open to enter leisurely. 'If I had minded,' he said mildly, 'I wouldn't have offered in the first place. Got any shampoo?'

'Er—it should be in the bathroom,' Nikki said, and whirled to go and look. Her shampoo and conditioner had been put on the shelf in the bath.

Harper had followed, and the tiny water closet became decidedly cramped. There was barely enough room for two bodies; when Nikki straightened with the bottles held gingerly, she brushed back against the hard length of Harper's body. His large hands, warm and strong, settled on the slim curve of her waist, then his fingers curled around her T-shirt and started to lift it.

Nikki's arms clamped to her sides, and she said breathlessly, 'I don't think that's necessary.'

'Sure it is. You don't want to get your clothes wet,' he chided, coaxing her arms up. His touch was a velvet slide against her highly sensitised skin, raising goose-bumps, and her body clenched against a betraying shudder. He asked, mockingly solicitous, 'What's the matter, don't you have a bra on?'

'That's not the point!' What a quandary she was in, dying to squirm at this powerfully sensual onslaught, and just too proud to give in. Her body felt as stiff as a board.

'Why don't you enlighten me, then?' he purred, his lips brushing her ear.

This was far more, both better and worse, than what she'd bargained for.

Harper took advantage—when did he not?—of her confusion and deftly edged the bright T-shirt over her black head. It sailed to the floor. Though she was wearing a bra, Nikki's arms folded across her chest in an instinctively protective manner. She watched out of the corner of her eye as he reached for a fluffy towel and handed it to her. She buried her hot face into it as he pushed her over to the waist-high sink and silently urged her to bend over it.

She bowed her neck in acquiescence, profoundly grateful that he could not see her face. She heard the gush of water, he guided her head under the warm flow, and the fingers of both his hands curled around her skull.

He shampooed her hair twice, then massaged conditioner into the wet locks, patient and thorough and stroking away the suds that crept down her slim neck. Nikki was in agony, face mashed against the dampening towel, her bare shoulders two slender wings to the graceful curve of her back. The chore lasted too long, and was over far too quickly as, with a decisiveness eloquent of some taut emotion, Harper snapped off the water flow abruptly, and threw the trailing ends of the towel over her wet head.

A waft of cool air drifted over her over-heated body, and Nikki knew that he had stepped away from her. Not daring to expose her burning complexion, she said, muffled, 'Thank you.'

'Don't mention it. I'll light a fire in the rear lounge, so that you can sit in front of it and let your hair dry.'

Harper was terse, clipped, totally at odds with the coaxing sensuality in his hands. She ventured to uncover one eye as she straightened, bewildered at his curious mood.

He was gone. She had heartily wished him gone in the midst of the uncomfortable intensity he had roused in her, but now that he was she felt an odd sense of anticlimax, as though all she had really wanted was for him to stay.

Which was ridiculous. She hadn't really wanted him to stay; of course she hadn't. Her problem was that she didn't know what she wanted. The issue got tangled up in a mass of conflicting urges that seemed to be tugging her first one way, then another.

She was still frowning ferociously as she stripped and, with a furtive sense of guilt, fished in her bag for the surgical rubber gloves the pharmacist had given her to protect her hands while she washed. With them, she could probably have managed her hair on her own. Nikki felt ludicrously as if she had cheated at a card game, and was relieved at not having been caught, as she carefully struggled into the gloves before stepping under the strong gush of water spray in the shower.

The intense warmth soaked into over-tense muscles, loosening them as it ran down the length of her body, and she sighed as she relaxed against one wall of the cubicle and leaned her head back.

Just what had she hoped to accomplish by her little stunt? What a marathon these last three days had been! And not just in terms of crisis and a stressful rejuggling of her schedule, but also the burgeoning of a whole wealth of unfamiliar thoughts and feelings, even down to this newest, most unwelcome worry that she had somehow misjudged Harper's attraction for her.

Not once after they had arrived in Oxford had he so much as hinted or referred to any of the things they had discussed—argued—spat at each other during the drive west. Not once had she caught even a glimpse of that unnerving, exciting, electric spark in his eyes whenever he looked at her, and she had begun to doubt every conclusion she had leapt to.

Perhaps he wasn't as attracted to her as she was to him. Perhaps even if he was, he was too wide and wise a person to act on it, and could concentrate instead on the positive aspects between them, such as her talent and their professional liaison, and their new budding friendship that was slowly beginning to take on shape and definition.

What, indeed, did she have as assets to attract someone as sophisticated and mature as Harper? Her critical gaze glanced down the slim curves and hollows of her glistening nude body with as much objectivity as she could achieve.

Her breasts were pert little mounds of pink-nippled flesh, no luscious sensuality there. The line of her torso dipped into an attractively tiny waist but did not flare into provocatively curved hips. The white skin over her thighs was smooth and unmarked; but her legs were tomboyishly slim as opposed to shapely, and as to the possible attractions of the dark curled triangle of femininity in the cradle of those unremarkable hips she could only shrug her shoulders in honest bewilderment.

Sexuality was a mystery to her in so many ways, but she was well aware that Harper was a very sexy man with a mature, wholesome appetite and a genuine warmth in his smile that brought her to tingling life every time he gave it to her. What was more, he had a vast capacity for tender nurturing that she could never have foreseen. One look at how he was with his nephew confirmed that. She had wondered if there was any decent substance behind the powerful businessman, and had got an answer that surpassed all her wildest dreams.

What did one do to pique the attention of a man like that? Frothy lingerie, scintillating conversation, worldly seductiveness? If so, she failed with flying colours.

Nikki finished washing and stepped out of the cubicle to dry herself with a roughness that turned her delicate skin bright red.

Her body had all the instincts of an adult woman, but she didn't know where that would lead her or what to do about it. She didn't know what the next stage was in the art of worldly seduction, and for the first time in her life felt that lack of knowledge as a drawback.

Certainly talking with Harper on the way to Oxford might have had just the warning effect she had originally intended, but she might have closed a door of possibility on herself by doing so.

When he'd had time to think about what she'd told him, might not he come to the conclusion that pursuing any further relationship with her was more trouble than it was worth? Would he see her warning as an outright rejection, and abide by that? Everything he had said and done so far since coming to Oxford seemed to point to one thing she was fast becoming sure of—that Harper was both decent and strong-willed enough to stick by his principles.

There seemed to be a rapid accumulation of barriers between Nikki and what she was beginning to accept that she wanted. With a defeated sigh, she trudged into her bedroom to pull on a very comfortable, criminally unexciting tracksuit and padded barefoot downstairs to partake of a relationship that was fast becoming bittersweet, for it was only half a loaf of bread.

CHAPTER FIVE

HARPER was sitting relaxed in an armchair by a crackling fire that banished the spring chill of evening from the rear lounge, in which a Bach concerto played over a superb stereo system. Nikki much preferred the somewhat shabby comfort of this smaller room to the elegant formality of the huge front reception area, and she hovered in the doorway for a moment of unnoticed observation.

He had that rare undefinable quality of being able to combine sternness with sensitive humanity, a tough male with an impressive presence that nevertheless could meld with his environment, not overshadow it. He had shed the Shetland sweater in the heat of the room and was now clad in simple shirt and jeans, the hard lines of his face softened into a tranquillity he had not exhibited in London. It was quite obvious just how much he loved his home.

One of the cats was in his lap, a striped orange, purring blanket of bliss. He raised one hand to stroke it absent-mindedly, the long, graceful line of his fingers outlined against the fire, and a shiver rippled down her spine as if she, too, had been stroked. How much easier it was to warm to this quieter side of his personality and abandon all the defences his ruthless side erected.

He turned his head and saw her, blue eyes somehow uncertain, her wet black hair standing up in untidy peaks, and all the emotion inside her gravitated towards him in a rush at the welcome in his smile. He lifted the cat off his lap to dump it without ceremony on the floor, and it hissed in fitful irritation before slinking off to wash out its disgust in a corner.

'There you are,' said Harper. 'Would you like me to pull over another armchair?'

She shook her head and walked over towards the fire, bare feet noiseless on the carpet. The warmth licked over her skin, melting away the chill that had begun to set in after her hot shower. 'I like sitting on the floor.'

'Come over here, in front of me,' he murmured, dark eyes reflecting the glow from the fire, gold swimming over liquid depths of cinnamon and coffee. 'Did you bring down a hairbrush? No? Never mind, I'll use my fingers. Your hair will dry in no time.'

That carried such an intense promise of sensual pleasure that her legs were already buckling by the time she had arrived in the indicated spot, with the result that her body collapsed into an untidy heap at his feet so ridiculously like a supplicant before a king that her face broke into self-derisive laughter. She was only thankful that her head was downbent so that she wouldn't have to explain the reason she was wearing such an idiotic expression.

Out of the frying-pan... She asked prosaically, 'Is Charles still in his room?'

'Yes, he's down for the night—a mixed blessing, as you'll no doubt find out for yourself, for we'll pay the price of having a peaceful evening by being awakened at an ungodly hour.' He had given her fair warning, and she had not rejected him, but still the light touch of his fingers threading throughout the short, wet strands of her hair to lift it sent a shock wave of sensation rippling through her. Her lips parted in a silent gasp that nevertheless betrayed her, for her body shuddered underneath his hand.

He said nothing, but continued to lift and separate the gleaming black locks in slow, gentle strokes until she vibrated with pleasure. Tension she hadn't even realised she'd had melted from her muscles until she felt boneless with delight, her head too heavy to hold upright. Her eyelids fell half closed; she didn't even notice how her head drooped to one side until the soft curve of her cheek connected with the denim-covered side of his knee. She jerked a little in surprise, but in instant sensitive reaction Harper's hand cupped the side of her head to forestall her instinctive effort to straighten.

Ah. She sighed. The moment was only fleeting, a murmurous flash of decision in which letting her body relax on to his legs was much the preferable option to forcing herself upright into rigid withdrawal, and down crept her cheek again to rest properly this time on his leg, and stay. Those hypnotic, magical fingers began to play through her hair once more.

'How do you like it here?' he asked.

'I love it,' she replied, in spontaneous honesty. 'You have a beautiful home.'

Her hair was dry. She could feel it; she was toasty warm all over. But still he stroked, and she couldn't have moved away from him for the world.

'So are you glad you came?'

'Mm. Yes, I am. I didn't realise it before, but I think I needed to get out of London for a while. This is all very refreshing.'

She could hear the smile in his voice as he asked her, 'And what about all your doubts?'

'Harper,' she said drily, stirring underneath his hand, 'I never did see you as a villain, otherwise I would have refused point blank to come, work or no work. What I was most concerned about was whether or not we could conduct our relationship with an honest integrity. I'm not into mind games.'

'No, you're not, are you?' he replied after a thoughtful moment. 'You say what you think, regardless of how difficult it is for you, or how it might prompt an adverse reaction. I admire that kind of courage. So you have no regrets?'

She smiled. 'I have many regrets, but coming here isn't one of them. Do you want to talk about work tomorrow, or would you rather do it tonight while Charles is in bed?'

'Have a heart,' he said with lazy amusement. 'It's my weekend, too. Let's just relax for the precious little time we can. Then, before I leave for London, I'll make sure that all the material you need to study is ready and waiting in the library on Monday morning. It'll wait until then, and I can call through the week to see how you're getting on, all right?'

She looked through her lashes at the dancing fire, blurred light and flickering shadow, and the long, stable length of Harper's leg stretched out beside her. 'All right. I just remembered,' she said and yawned. 'Would you mind if I let Peter know your phone number, so that he can contact me if he needs to?'

'I don't mind, as long as he's discreet.' The deep voice was very soft, followed by his forefinger tracing the delicate curve of her ear. It tickled so much that she twitched and reached up to clap a hand over her ear, to which he chuckled and squeezed her fingers in wordless apology.

'Peter can be very discreet, especially when there's profit involved,' she told him ironically, and he laughed.

'But of course I won't tell him, if you don't want me to.'

'That would be churlish of me. The poor man would be frantic if he didn't know where to contact you. I'm content to trust your judgement. If you say he's discreet, then I'll believe he is unless he proves otherwise, which wouldn't be difficult. Not very many people have my Oxford home number.'

He had resumed those slow, gentle finger strokes through her hair, watching the dark, gleaming head as it rested on his knee. Nikki's small bandaged hand slid away from her ear, revealing the long, vulnerable beauty of her curved neckline. Her skin was ivory-white and blue-shadowed, and he could just see the tiny beat of her pulse fluttering beneath the slim feminine jaw, as delicate as the beat of a butterfly wing.

'You're very protective of your home,' she murmured, eyelids drooping.

'I have to be. I shelter some precious things here, and I am, as you so pungently pointed out yesterday, too rich, and too well-known, and sometimes attract some very unwelcome attention.' And despite the fortune in artwork and furnishings that decorated his house the very quality of his voice was such that Nikki knew he did not refer to material objects.

'I'm a protector, not a destroyer.' That was what he had said earlier in the car, and she began to have a sense of how completely he had meant it. He would watch over the people that meant a lot to him, compulsively, quietly, with a sharp eye to every detail even down to knowing the name of everybody who possessed his personal phone number.

That sort of unceasing diligence could have prompted in Nikki a sense of claustrophobia, but somehow it didn't. She knew from first-hand experience how fatal it could be to assume that tragedy only happened to someone else; would her father be alive today had he taken more precautions instead of believing in his own myth of invincibility? The golden era of her youth had been an illusion, she realised, where everyone had been slightly drunk on the power drug.

Here and now was a different story. From earlier conversations, and from what she had just gleaned from him right then, she could see that Harper knew the uses and abuses of power so well that he kept the two halves of his life completely separate so that the private side was not influenced or damaged in any way by the public. It was no wonder she had begun to feel safe, deeply, instinctively safe in a way that she hadn't since before her father died, and the adult inside her recognised it as a far more stable quality than that of her youth.

'Has Charles ever seen your house in Mayfair?' she asked in sudden apparent irrelevance.

Rueful respect threaded through Harper's voice as he replied, 'You never fail to see every nuance, do you? No, he's never been to my house in Mayfair. Neither have Anne, or Gavin, or my mother or a whole circle of my friends. Gordon has; you have. Before she died, my sister used to come to London for the odd visit. Precious few see both halves of my life, let alone understand them.'

At last Nikki let her eyelids close, for they were simply too heavy. Surreptitiously she rubbed her cheek against the hard knee pillowing her head and murmured, 'Don't you find it a strain?'

'I find it a necessity,' he responded briefly, and she made a drowsy murmur of sympathy.

Drowsy? Nikki's eyes fluttered open in surprise. Oh, surely not drowsy; she'd never sleep the first evening in a strange place in the company of a man who charged her up. Relaxed, that was what she was. It lapped at the edges of her consciousness, soothing a body already warm and content. Instead of fighting the relaxation, she let go.

'How amazing,' she murmured, as the fire and the shadows came together and melded. Everything was suddenly very clear to her.

He waited, but when she did not continue, he asked, stroking the hair from her brow, 'What's amazing?'

Nikki didn't answer. She was sound asleep.

Harper sat for some time bathed in firelight as he watched the dark head on his knee. Then he stirred, and with patient gentleness bent to ease his arms underneath her slumbering, lax body and lift her on to his lap. Her only protest was a deep sound, halfway between a sigh and a light snore, as he slid his hand around the back of her skull to guide her head on to the broad support of his shoulder.

She looked like a child as he held her, the clear, translucent skin across her cheekbones flushed with warmth and sleep. She looked all woman, from the lush curves of her relaxed, parted lips to the softness of her body as she snuggled instinctively against him into a more comfortable position.

He thought no one was watching him, but he was wrong. After checking one last time on Charles, the housekeeper Anne made her way through the downstairs hall. She paused on the threshold of the rear lounge, having intended to ask if Harper wanted anything else before she retired for the night, but the question went unuttered as Anne saw him press a tender kiss to Nikki's forehead. She saw, too, the look on his face as he cradled the young girl.

* * *

Nikki opened her eyes and stared at the roses on the ceiling. That was just too odd. She blinked; the roses remained, and after a few more moments of confusion she finally attached them to the canopy of the four-poster bed, not the ceiling. The ceiling was a plain sober white, she was in the four-poster bed, and the sun was high in the sky by the look of things outside her balcony door.

Heavens to Betsy, she'd overslept! Nikki thought about smiling from sheer refreshment, but she frowned instead. She didn't remember how she had got to bed. All she remembered was how surprised she felt at the realisation that she was falling asleep, as she stared at the flames and Harper stroked her hair—downstairs.

He must have brought her up and tucked her into bed. She checked her body underneath the covers, her face flooding with intense colour. How sweet of him, how like the night in London, how—embarrassing. He had removed the trousers of her tracksuit so that she wore only her sweatshirt and knickers. What had run through his mind as he had eased the soft grey material over her slim legs with those clever, sensitive fingers?

'You have lovely legs.' A stab of sheer physical longing pierced through her; she didn't know how to assuage it, but she knew that Harper did.

She remembered the gentleness of his hands, and the warmth from the fire, and how they had talked, and she remembered too how safe she had felt with him, and how the very quality of that safety had filtered through her mind and body.

Nikki stretched, feeling her body slide under the weight of the blankets. How wonderful she felt, how exotic and yet familiar. A stealthy noise came from her bedroom door, and Nikki turned her head to watch lazily as her doorknob twisted around. The door was pushed open with a great deal of stealth, and Charles's dark, curious head poked around the corner of it. When he saw Nikki's wide-awake, quizzical blue eyes on him, he made a strangled sound and ducked back out so that she laughed out loud and called for him to come in.

The boy sidled in, clad in thoroughly disreputable jeans and oversized shirt. He begged her, 'Harper warned me not to disturb you, but I thought I'd check to see if you were already awake—you won't tell, will you?'

'Of course not,' replied Nikki as she propped herself up on her pillows. 'Anyway, you haven't disturbed me, I was already awake just as you thought I might be. What time is it?'

'Almost noon,' he told her, with a hint of reproof as he threw himself on to the bottom of her bed. 'You've slept through the morning. My grandmother's here. She likes to be called Helena, that's why I call her Granny.'

Nikki's laugh bubbled out again. 'Do you? And what does she do?'

He grinned. 'She holds her mouth tight and looks down her nose at me.'

'Well,' Nikki said with mock severity, 'I can see I'll have to watch myself around you! Why don't you go downstairs now, so that I can get dressed? I'll be down soon.'

He grumbled but complied, throwing over one thin shoulder carelessly, 'I'll tell Anne you're up. Want any breakfast?'

Not wanting to be any trouble, Nikki said, 'No, thanks, but I'd love some tea. I'll be down in fifteen minutes.'

She was skipping down the stairs in ten, dressed in a plain cream blouse, an embroidered waistcoat and tan trousers. After her deep, dreamless sleep she looked lively, buoyant, her blue eyes sparkling with vitality.

She decided to go to the kitchen in search of her cup of tea, and ran into Harper as she rounded the corner. Both his hands shot out to catch and steady her as she rocked on her feet. She looked from the broad expanse of chest in front of her eyes straight up to his face, exclaiming with a laugh, 'We seem to make a habit of colliding into one another——'

Her voice died away as their eyes met, and sizzled. It was like tapping into an insulated electrical current; everything in the world stayed completely normal while she heated up and fried under the intensity of his midnight-dark gaze. The serenity of their evening in front of the fire was gone, blown up in the silent explosion. Could this have been what he felt when he put her to bed, easing her clothing away from soft, slim thighs, slipping her between the private sheets? Her lips parted, eyes stunned as they clung to him, dilating into reflecting brilliant black.

Oh, how wrong could she be? Oh, how could she have imagined such a magnitude of sexual interplay tossing in the turbulent chocolate ocean of his eyes? One blink and Harper was nothing more than friendly, his hand lingering no more than necessary to make sure she had her balance, a light smile creasing his lean, handsome face for her tempestuous entrance.

She felt bereft and grieving for what had only been a betrayal of her own wishful thinking, and yet had seemed so real for a moment when she could almost have believed that he would greet her with passionate gladness. Instead he reached out with a brotherly hand to rumple her hair and say, much as he would to Charles, 'Hello there, you must have slept well. I'll introduce you to my mother after you've had your breakfast. Anne's just cooking you up something now.'

She averted her face sharply, nostrils flared with an attempt to control a stupid, stupid urge to lash out and hit him. 'I'd better go on back, then,' she said tightly.

He ducked his head in an effort to see her downbent face, where all the vitality had drained away, and asked with a sharp frown, 'Are you all right?'

She threw her head back and smiled at him brilliantly. 'Of course I'm all right; why wouldn't I be?'

'I don't know,' he said in a soft, thoughtful voice, and she knew she had to leave fast.

'What a pal you were to tuck me into bed last night,' she told him, reaching up to pat his cheek as she danced around him. Harper's grey head reared back as sharply as if she had indeed struck him, and something very like anger flared in those hard, fierce eyes, but Nikki had not lingered in the hall to witness it.

At the kitchen table Anne set in front of her a complete English breakfast, and, much to her surprise, Nikki ate it. But the flavour seemed absent from both the food and the day, burned away in the heat of a moment. She would not brood; she instead concentrated on all five animals begging at her feet, on Anne, on Charles as distractions. Later, when she was introduced to the slim, elegant, white-haired Helena Beaumont, Nikki concentrated on her.

The older woman was very much reserved but impeccably polite, and fragile in a way that was totally unlike the steel quality of strength inherent in Harper and growing in Charles. Nikki could just imagine the frail English rose beauty Helena Beaumont must have been in her youth. As the afternoon progressed the older woman seemed to unbend considerably, almost in direct contrast to the increasing tension Nikki sensed building underneath Harper's smooth, sociable façade.

But she wouldn't focus on him. Every time their eyes came close to meeting, Nikki's slid away from the contact, afraid that he would intuit the severe sense of deprivation she felt in his company. Everything about her response to him that Sunday afternoon was quicksilver, half averted. She was being, as he was, so friendly, so polite, so inaccessible.

When at last Helena had bidden them all goodbye that evening after supper, exclaiming that she had stayed much later than she had intended, Nikki slipped away from Harper while Charles still provided some distraction.

She fled up the stairs and into her room to collapse on her bed. What was so wrong with her that she couldn't even behave naturally around him? So what if her imagination ran riot whenever he so much as touched her? So what if he treated her with a simple friendliness— why should that scour such an abrasive path through her? She had to get herself under some kind of control. She had to get some fresh air. Nikki thrust off her bed, and went to fumble for the catch on her balcony door.

A cool breeze puffed like a sigh on to her overheated skin as she stepped out into the night. The Oxford sky was different from London's. There wasn't as much light pollution, and even the air smelled cleaner. She went to the railing and leaned against it, breathing in deeply the scent of flowers and newly cut grass, and rich, fresh-tilled earth while her galloping heart began to slow. Light from the bedroom behind her fell half across her body and on to the ground below, cutting a swath through the dark evening.

She didn't know if she could sort through the tangled mess of confusion inside her, but she did know one thing. If she didn't get a strong hold on herself, and soon, Harper was going to remark on it, and then what would she tell him? She didn't want to tell him the truth, and he'd know if she didn't. With any luck, she thought, he wouldn't comment on the strangeness of their interaction today.

As it happened, however, Nikki was fresh out of luck.

CHAPTER SIX

THE first indication of Nikki's luck running out was the velvet purr of a voice, coming out of the shadow from her left. 'I wondered if you would be out here.'

Nikki practically leapt out of her skin, whirled and gasped, with one hand to her pulsating throat, 'How did you get out here? Where are you?'

A deeper shadow detached itself from the others, so thoroughly unnerving in silence, liquid movements of solid bone, muscled awareness, intention. Harper murmured, 'I came out through my bedroom door, and I am right in front of you.'

She was pressed against the railing so hard that the metal barrier bit into her back, but she never realised it. All her attention was focused on his materialisation. One more step and the reflected light from her room caught at the grey hair, the bright, dark eyes, the tough line of his cheek and the elegant curve of that stern mouth.

The next step and his sexy mouth was smiling. The next step and the bulk of his powerful body leapt into illumination. Nikki's blue eyes were frantic. She looked everywhere fast, for she didn't know where to look, and finally she settled the whole idiotic dilemma by turning to lean her elbows on the railing and stare down at the shadowed grass. The silhouette of her head was in the rectangle of light thrown over the lawn, and she watched as a taller, broader silhouette joined her.

'I didn't know the balcony was so long,' she whispered.

'You've never been out here before, and Charles's guided tour of the grounds yesterday couldn't have given you much time for proper observation. Most of the bedrooms share a balcony, except for the front ones. Nikki, why have you been avoiding me today?'

His arm brushed her shoulder as he leaned on the railing beside her, those large, strong hands loosely clasped. She turned her head to look at nothing in particular, just to hide her face. 'I wasn't aware that I had avoided you.'

'Don't lie to me.' If the cool containment earlier in his voice was devastating, the quiet snarl that followed it was immeasurably so. 'I can respect it if you honestly don't want to answer, but I cannot respect a lie.'

'I'm not lying!' she felt goaded into exclaiming. 'I never avoided you! In fact, I tried very hard all day to behave just as you were behaving towards me! I'm sorry if I didn't manage to achieve quite the same effect— obviously I'm not as good at this as you are!'

She heard it, a tiny shocking sound, as he drew in a harsh, shaken breath. When she glanced back at him quickly, she found his face was grim and downbent. 'Of course you are talking about earlier this morning, when we bumped into each other in the hall. My God,' said Harper, in which she read a curious combination of furious resignation and frustrated disgust, 'do you ever miss a trick?'

'I might not miss them, but I don't always understand them,' she replied, voice trembling in bitterness. 'You were so perfectly cool and composed, I thought the whole thing was my over-active imagination, and desperately tried to cover it up. You've got me so mixed up, I don't know which way to turn.'

'Don't you think I know that?' he growled, his body vibrating with violent tension. He turned his head and hard, angry eyes stabbed her. 'We might as well air the whole damned mess, since this appears to be confession time——'

'Don't throw my father back in my face!' she exploded in warning, and the brief release of tension felt wonderful.

'No, let's talk about your inexperience instead!' he shot back with such dreadful accuracy that she flinched and almost cried. Damn him, he did know her, better than she knew herself, only this was such a private insecurity that she couldn't bear it. As if in spite of himself, his voice gentled. 'Shall I lay it out for you? We have known each other three days, and already we have established something rare. Isn't that so?'

'Yes,' she whispered, but she pulled away from him when he would have reached out to grasp her hand.

If anything Harper became even more gentle, and how it hurt her. 'You know I'm attracted to you. You're too clever and perceptive for me to hide it. Isn't that so?'

'Yes,' she whispered again, and she almost hated him, for she could sense what was coming.

He looked straight ahead of him with a fierce frown, and his profile was everything hard and determined, cut from stone, all spontaneity bled away. 'And you. Strike at me if you must, but you are so innocent, like a child inside a woman's unawakened body. How could you know how to interpret the signals between us, or how to react to your feelings, or even, I suspect, what it is you want? But I told you already, nothing is going to happen between us that you don't want. I am trying, dammit, to make things easier for you, not to add to your confusion.'

If she had not invested so much of herself into the conversation, perhaps she might have been able to appreciate his effort at patience and understanding, but Nikki was not about to try to disassociate herself. The bottom line was that this hurt. He hurt her. He reached into her heart and told her what was there, and the worst, most terrible part of it was that he did so dispassionately.

'What a brilliant theorist you are!' she exclaimed, eyes flashing with blue fire. 'And what a shame, but, for your information, I am a person, not a mathematical problem that can be solved by laying everything out in straight, defined rows! Weren't you the one who said life can't be pigeon-holed the way we would like it? Do you know what your trouble is? Not only are you too perceptive as well, but you are too accustomed to assuming responsibility. Well, I don't care if you can outguess me, but I won't let you take responsibility for my thoughts and feelings!'

'For God's sake, what would you have me do?' he snapped, gripping at the railing with both hands until they were bone-white. 'Every time I get near you, you're like a panicked bird, but when I try to be gentle you go for my throat!'

Tears of sheer fury, tears of pain sprang to her eyes and spilled over, and it was such a destructive combination of emotion that she threw herself into the heart of it and cried, 'Let's take it one step further! Obviously my inexperience here is a problem! Perhaps I should just take my *inexperience* some place else. Somebody ought to be kind enough to rid me of it, and then maybe I'll be able to meet you at your own level of sophisticated expertise!'

She had pierced him right past all his armour to the quick, and touched the volcano of reaction he had hidden inside. He rounded on her, making a raw, animalistic sound at the back of his throat. His face was frightening as he grabbed her by the shoulders, and she bent backwards under his strength like a reed before a whirlwind storm. 'Don't talk like that—don't *ever* talk like that!' he bit out, shaking her hard.

But once she had started she couldn't stop, and snapped, 'Well, that's the trick, isn't it? If only you'd stop sending me crossed signals and make up your mind, maybe I'd know how to react! But obviously you want me the way you want me, not for who I really am!'

'You haven't the slightest clue how I want you!' He breathed the words almost soundlessly, all his anger gone into the taut shape of his mouth, the hardened clench of his jawline, the explosion spilling out of his eyes. He towered over her, pure, rampant aggression, so utterly, impossibly powerful that her head fell back. The slim, feminine curves of her throat were suddenly outlined in stark, revealing light.

'Well,' she whispered in shaky reaction, 'how very interesting.'

He was faster than anyone she had ever met. Dark, hard eyes flared with incredulity and fury, but this time it was bitten back and held. 'I shall give you fair warning, Nikki,' said Harper softly, almost gently, 'which is more than I have ever given to anyone else. Don't ever try to manipulate or provoke me again.'

'Not even to clear the air?' she asked, insouciantly.

'My God,' he uttered, sexy mouth shaped around bared teeth, 'you need taming.'

'Oh, I hope not,' she retorted before she could help herself. Did she mean it in taunting reply, or in fearful exclamation? 'But then I hear powerful men prefer docility.'

As the insolent words resounded in the air around them, she stood petrified. That's torn it. She'd pushed him too far this time.

He snarled and hauled her against his chest, violent and intent and never so well directed as he was then, threading both big hands through the hair at the back of her head, dragging her face up, his eyes two great, eruptive black pools as they focused on her soft, vulnerable mouth. She had just a split-second of blank astonishment, a vast suspense poised on the brink of a precipice, and then his head swooped down like a striking hawk, and she was shattered, everything was shattered, and in the next instant remade.

It was, as nothing else could be, a baptism of fire. It scorched her to the bone and seared her soul. It was the first and only kiss, a conflagration, a death indeed of innocence, and at the same time a shrieking phoenix flight, for nothing was spared or held back as he kissed her with full unbridled passion, ravenous and openmouthed, penetrating her with his tongue and plunging her headlong into deepest adult sensuality. The last of her childhood blew away in butterfly tatters before the ravaging male, and the unawakened woman inside her stirred, and opened her eyes.

He might have drawn back at some point, were it not for the deep, reactive moan she gave into his mouth like purest wine, the shudder that swept her from head to foot, unbearably intoxicating against his body, the exquisite tremor in those slim arms she raised to drape around his neck.

He felt her fingers in his hair, clumsy with greed, the incredible softness of her mouth moving under his, the unexpected savagery that took over inside him as he bit those lush, fruitful lips, and her own gasp before she bit him back in retaliation, not as delicately as he, nowhere as experienced as he, not experienced at all but for this—and this—and this——

With each urgent thrust of his tongue, she felt an answering stab of pure agonised pleasure rocket through her body, which seemed to have a mind of its own but for her full conscious agreement. Her body was wiser than she, as her knees collapsed and, with a groan, he wrapped his tough, strong arms even tighter around her, thighs flush on trembling thighs, hip to hip, breasts pressed to masculine, heart-racing chest. Her body was wiser again, as it came in contact with a full throbbing aggression pressed against the pit of her stomach and writhed, leaving her bewildered mind to catch up belatedly as he gave a sharp gasp, then held tight to both hips and thrust against her.

Oh, my lord, of course. Her blind blue eyes stared up at the night sky, head cradled in the cup of one hand as he sweetly, hotly ravaged down the side of her neck. The other hand he brought up to rake lightly across the tip of her breast, a lightning-quick plundering that brought her to a shivering fever pitch. His fullness, her aching emptiness; his plundering, her enticement, his aggressive need, oh, how she needed.

As if in echo, he groaned against her ear, 'For God's sake, Nikki!'

'I know!' she cried hotly, burying her face into the abundant grey hair that was so much softer than she had imagined. 'But I don't know what to do!'

He froze, panting, just held her tight while the stroke of his heartbeat thudded into her like the heavy stroke of a bronze gong, then slowly came the most agonising part of all as his arms loosened in torturous withdrawal. 'No, you don't know what to do,' whispered Harper, and it would have destroyed her except that he had managed even then to reach past passion to tenderness. 'You don't even know how to use birth control, do you, darling? And here I am, the sophisticated, mature man who would have lain you down right here and taken you in spite of it.'

He let go of her, stepped back, hands clenched into fists at his sides, and when she would have touched his face he recoiled as if lashed by a whip, whispering through bloodless lips, 'As you value your safety, don't touch me now.'

He stared as she flinched, and she felt when it ran over her and read what she knew to be there. Eyes too dilated, for the light was too bright; lips too swollen, for how they pulsed; skin too flushed, for she was burning inside like a torch.

In fact she must look much as he looked, and, heavens, it was a case of either throwing a screaming tantrum to relieve the terrible pressure, or laugh, and she was so busy trying to make up her mind between the two that she was totally unprepared for how he pivoted sharply on one heel and strode away. He threw over one shoulder, very quietly as he melted into insubstantial shadow, 'Goodnight, Nikki.'

That's it? she wanted to shriek, and in fact, as the air resounded, realised she had. Harper's voice came to her, with the amusement she hadn't achieved, 'Darling, that isn't the half of it, but it's more than enough, I think, for now.'

She heard it quite distinctly, the latch of his balcony door clicking into place as he shut it behind him, and her world tumbled around her eyes with a crash, going from ecstatic eroticism to frustrated pique in what must have broken the world record for the swiftness of mood swings.

He was so horribly well-adjusted, so fiendishly considerate, so damned right! Of course he would not take her right then and there; they had all the rotten time in the world. Oh, she wanted to kill him!

And she knew, naturally, that she wanted to do no such thing. She knew exactly what she wanted, and had been denied for all the best of intentions, and for all she knew might never be offered again, and she knew as well that laughter had no place in this desperate let-down.

And she had been concerned only a lifetime ago yesterday about how he would behave when they got here. Harper had behaved like a gentleman. Nikki stalked into her room, threw herself on to her bed, buried her head deep into a soft pillow and screamed out her rage of frustration and anguish. And, as if that weren't enough impetuosity, she had to top it all off by bursting into tears.

She told herself she wanted to die, but she fell asleep instead.

Some time between the night and the morning Nikki burrowed her way underneath the heavy blankets, and for the second time in a row woke up to disorientation. She was still in the clothes she had donned yesterday, and they had become extremely uncomfortable.

The memory of last night seared her mind's eye even as she came to the belated realisation of what had disturbed her sleep. The knock on her door had been light and unobtrusive; if she hadn't been so close to waking anyway she would have slept right through it.

She stretched and rolled over with a huge yawn, and called out in a sleep-blurred voice, 'Come in.'

She had expected Charles, but the door opened on Harper instead.

He was dressed in a tailored grey suit, the sleek severity of which emphasised the breadth of shoulders and lean hips. He looked aggressive and sophisticated, and dangerously attractive. Nikki bolted into a sitting position, her eyes large and self-conscious for her rumpled state. At the best of times Harper was unsettling; at that time, when she was relaxed and undefended, the impact of his presence hit her like a brick.

His eyes ran leisurely over her and a slow, smoky smile creased his face. 'Oh, dear,' he said with mock chagrin, 'did I wake you up?'

An answering smile, sweet and malicious, spread across her lips. 'Yes,' she told him limpidly, 'you did. My, I must have slept like a rock. I don't remember a thing once my head hit the pillow. How did you sleep?'

She had meant to wipe his smile away; instead it deepened with amusement. 'Very well, thank you,' he murmured, excessively polite, as he thrust open the door and strolled into the room.

'Was there anything in particular you wanted?'

He laughed at her very gently. Nikki's malice scampered out of her head as she flushed a very deep red. Her traitorous tongue; she should have it cut out at the earliest opportunity. 'Only to say goodbye,' replied Harper, halting at the side of the bed. 'I'm off to London. The material you need to look over is on my desk downstairs. I'll call in the week to see how things are going.'

'Fine,' she said tightly, vibrating with the urge to shift under his penetrating stare. The back of her neck was beaded with moisture.

He bent over her and tilted up her unresisting chin with one long finger. 'Well, Nikki, visiting with you has certainly been—stimulating,' he murmured. 'So sorry to kiss and run. Miss me just a little?'

Damn it, her skin was so thin; what would it take to get under his and wipe that unholy expression off his face? An evil genius prompted her to say innocently, as she opened her eyes very wide, 'But of course—who else will tuck me in at night?'

She saw the heat that darkened his skin and simmered in his eyes, and her triumph backfired on her, as she was helpless to control her own reaction. 'Hold that thought,' he advised, planting a swift, hard kiss on her softened mouth. He pivoted on one heel, neat as a dancer, and exited the room.

Nikki expelled an explosive breath and fell back against her pillows, as limp as if she'd just run a marathon. She felt again that incredible throb of physical hunger, an empty, barren ache that was actual pain. How amazing and disturbing, and how badly she needed to think this through.

It transpired that Charles had already gone complaining off to his school and wouldn't be seen again until later that afternoon. Anne's husband Gavin was mysteriously busy in the flat above the garage, and Nikki found, as the housekeeper fixed her another huge breakfast which she polished off almost guiltily, that the resulting peace in the house echoed with emptiness.

At first time weighed heavily on her hands and she moped, but then as the week progressed she began to get a sense of balance for the freedom from her usually hectic schedule. It became a freedom to think ahead, and plan, and sort out just what the significance was of the last week, and also come to terms with Harper's appearance in her life.

She went through a whole gamut of intense emotions, including rejection, but finally arrived at an honest conclusion. Harper had fast become so important that she was willing to endure the sometimes terrible sense of exposure she felt around him. Just how important he was, she couldn't say yet; she only knew that her life would seem empty now without him.

She found herself filing away incidences, little snippets of gossip, ridiculous things Charles said, as she thought to herself, I must tell Harper about this. And then she immediately told herself not to be stupid. He was far too busy to be interested in such unimportant trivialities.

But when, over the phone, he asked her about her day and she found herself telling him, and she heard the warm, delicious sound of his laughter break through the terse, glacial distance that had built up around him in London, she knew she had been wrong. He was vitally interested. London was only his power base, and he missed his home.

Each morning she woke up bounding with energy. She gobbled up the huge stack of concise information Harper had left for her and began to make preliminary plans for new designs.

She called Peter, who called her back three times, visited a local doctor blushingly to eradicate the latest barrier Harper had thrown in her face on Sunday, abandoned the dressings over her hands as the cuts closed for good, and, after receiving Harper's amused approval, took Charles several times into Oxford for a bit of sightseeing and shopping.

Charles was an amazing shopping companion. He had very definite ideas about what he would wear and picked out several summer outfits for himself, but what she hadn't expected was for the six-year-old to be so patient and enthusiastic about her needs and desires. As Nikki recalled, her brother Johnny had been nothing of the sort. But Charles was, in fact, quite fashion-conscious and possessed an inherent sense of good taste.

Once, when she hovered thoughtfully over a tight-waisted, full-skirted green dress, Charles remarked very casually, 'Harper doesn't like green.'

Nikki's startled gaze flashed to the boy's dark eyes. He knew what she was up to, all right; it was written all over his thin young face, and if he had smirked at the thought she would have wanted to hit him. But Charles's irrepressible smile was conspiratorial, his expression one of a gleeful accomplice. She realised then that she had his full seal of approval, unlooked and unasked for, and she surprised them both by throwing her arms around his small, sturdy body.

Again he amazed her for he giggled, the worldly young man collapsing giddily into the child, and he hugged her back. It was then that she knew with quite simple amazement that not only had she fallen madly in love with the older Beaumont, but she loved the younger one as well.

By Friday morning she had recovered so much mobility in her hands that she'd already begun to make sketches of the various designs Harper required. She worked in the library, over the large table which was littered with papers and pencils, and the various examples of the outdated material his company had formerly produced.

Charles was home that day due to school closures for teacher training, and instead of roaming about outside in the sunshine seemed quite content to mimic Nikki.

He was sprawled underneath the table, with several sheafs of the paper she had given him, scribbling busily with his crayons, dark head bent intently over the spaceship he was drawing.

Loath as she was to disrupt the serenity of the morning, Nikki decided over lunch that she had to go into town again for better art materials. 'I need to pick up some pens and watercolours, and the right kind of paper so that I can do my sketches properly,' she told Anne. 'Do you know a shop where I can buy them?'

'Try Broad Street in town,' said the housekeeper after a moment's frowning thought. 'I think there's an art shop along there somewhere.'

Charles was munching on an American-style hamburger, a glass of chocolate milk beside his plate, while he kicked incessantly at the legs of his chair. 'I need some pens as well,' he hinted slyly, to which Nikki laughed.

'Oh, do you? What happened to your crayons?'

'They're for babies,' he said in disgust, then fixed her with a bright, pleading glance. 'Can I come too? I have money, three whole pounds.'

'I thought you were saving that for a skateboard,' she said, having already heard Harper's pithy opinion on that subject earlier in the week.

'I want pens,' said the boy stubbornly. Monkey see, monkey do, she thought with a smile, and as it was by far the safer of his two desires she acquiesced readily. Charles whooped with delight and wolfed down the rest of his burger, and soon after they headed out into the bright afternoon.

It was a perfect chance to kill two birds with one stone, she thought as they waited for the next bus into town. She really did need the art supplies, for all her things were back in her bed-sit in London, and now she could keep busy with her pride intact until Harper arrived some time that evening, for she couldn't wait to see him again. To look in his face, to see his smile, to want so desperately to throw herself into his arms—that fierce, disturbing ache which was both emotional and physical, built to an unbearable pitch at the very thought of him, and if she hung around the house all afternoon and did nothing she would be bound to make a fool of herself.

Oxford was beginning to fill up with summer tourists, and as the streets were clogged with people and traffic it took far longer than she had first anticipated to get to Broad Street and find the shop they wanted. Somehow what was supposed to be a simple expedition for pens and art supplies turned into a search for comic books and ice-cream as well, which turned into a very messy business in the heat of the day, so that when Nikki was at last scouring the shelves in the art shop the sun had advanced unnoticed across the wide, cloudless sky.

Charles had happily found a corner of the shop where he could sit on the floor and pore over his comic books. She kept a close eye on him while she moved about the shop, but he seemed content enough to wait however long it took her to pick out the materials she needed.

She was studying the various sizes of watercolour paper in supply, and mentally trying to work out just how much of each she might need, when a dark shadow fell across her line of vision, and she murmured, 'Would you mind not standing in my light, please?'

'But, my love, I've been standing to one side for the last ten minutes in the hope that you'd look up,' replied a deep familiar voice that splintered her absorption.

Instantly all thought, common sense, and restraint were scattered as well, as Nikki dropped the paper, whirled in an upsurge of uncontrollable gladness and flung herself at Harper. He grunted at the moment her slender body made impact with his, both his hard arms closing around her, and it was such extraordinary, perfect bliss—and in the next instant her face flooded with dismay and she stepped back.

He gave her a cool little smile as he let her go at once. 'Of the two, I think I much prefer your first reaction,' he said lightly.

But Nikki was in the throes of deep contrition. 'I'm so sorry,' she babbled, her hands hovering as if to try wiping away the damp pink spot she had smeared on his very expensive business suit. 'We bought ice-cream, and Charles's was strawberry flavoured, and there was a slight accident, and now I've got it on you as well!'

'So I see,' he remarked, his face unreadable as he looked from her down to the bent head of the boy sitting on the floor in one corner. Charles still hadn't noticed Harper, but was lost in a world of his own, one filled with bright colours and dramatic pictures, and inter-galactic heroes winning battles over supervillains. He looked dishevelled, dirty, smeared with ice-cream much as Nikki was, and extremely happy.

Nikki looked as well, but all she saw was how filthy Charles had managed to get, and sudden worry rose up inside for what sort of impression the man beside her might be gleaning from the picture. If he thought she wasn't looking after the boy properly, he might not let her take Charles out again, and she said with quick anxiety, 'He did have a good lunch before we came out.'

'I'm sure he did,' replied Harper, turning to stare at her curiously.

'And I'm sorry,' she continued in a rush, 'I don't know how he managed to get so dirty, but——'

'Snips and snails and puppydogs' tails,' he said, and laughed. 'You haven't seen him yet when he goes out into the back garden to play in the rain. This, by comparison, is next to godliness. Besides, my love, have you by any chance had a look at yourself in a mirror recently?'

She glanced down at her smudged jeans and blouse and closed her eyes in deep chagrin. She must look even worse next to Harper's cultured masculinity, his grey hair sleek and his stern face handsome. She thought of the peacock-blue silk dress she had expected to greet him in that very evening, of what an utter and transparent fool she must have appeared when she had thrown herself into his arms, and felt justifiably bitter.

His interest had quickened at the darkness that had clouded her face; she sensed it and, partly in truth, partly because she wanted to cover up her deeper reactions, she said quietly, 'I'm just worried that you might think I haven't been looking after him properly when I take him out.'

'Worried!' he echoed, his strange expression intensifying. 'Whatever put that idea in your head? Every time I've called home this last week, Charles has done nothing but talk about what you and he have done together.'

She asked humbly, her blue eyes huge, 'Do you mind?'

'Darling,' he said, lifting one hand to pass it over her hair in a feather-light stroke, 'I'm delighted you're getting along with him so well. I couldn't have hoped for anything better.'

She glanced at her feet, then up again, a swift, shy look as she made the helpless confession, 'I adore him.'

The smile that broke over Harper's face transformed him completely. The expression in his dark eyes was open, and very gentle, and lit from within. He said very softly, 'I love him too.'

'Harper!' The exclamation came from Charles, who had at last looked up from his comic book and noticed them. The boy waved a grubby, excited hand. 'Look what I got!'

'In a moment, sport.' Harper glanced at the shopping basket at Nikki's feet and asked, 'Are you done here?'

'Almost,' she said, her attention shifting with reluctance to what had so preoccupied her just a little while before. 'I just have to choose the paper I want, and pay for all this. I've started on some rough ideas for you, but of course we need to discuss quite a lot of it.'

'Good, you can show them to me over the weekend. Go ahead and finish what you were doing; there's no hurry.' With that, he strolled over to Charles and bent to look over the comics and pens the boy clutched.

Nikki's concentration had completely disintegrated, however, and she could no longer remember how many sketches of which size she had intended to make. She made a quick, arbitrary selection, gathered everything together and went to the cash till to pay.

Harper wouldn't let her, though, insisting on settling the bill himself. After all, he pointed out reasonably when she would have argued, she wouldn't have needed to buy the things had she been back in her studio in London. After a moment's struggle, she gave in as gracefully as she could, and with Charles holding their hands as he skipped between them Harper guided them to where he'd parked his car.

'Anne must have told you where to find us,' Nikki commented as he unlocked the doors.

'Yes, I thought I'd come looking for you two, because I wanted to give you fair warning about our imminent weekend guests.'

'Terrific,' muttered an antisocial Charles from the back.

Nikki admitted, in her secret heart of hearts, to the same sense of intrusion, which was wholly uncalled for, considering that not only was she herself a guest, but Harper had warned her from the beginning of the possibility of other visitors. Once she had welcomed the thought.

Now Harper said, with a smiling glance in the rearview mirror, 'Oh, it's not so bad, sport. It's just Gordon, and Gayle.'

'That's all right, then,' said the wriggling boy.

'So nice to have your approval,' replied Harper in a dry voice, at which Nikki laughed silently. Then he said to her, 'Gordon's dying to see you again, and Gayle Chancellor is a mutual friend of ours who goes way back. Ah, I see they've already arrived.'

That last was as they turned into the drive where a lemon-yellow Mercedes sports coupé was parked in front of the house. A couple were just climbing out, equally polished and beautiful, like a matched set of Dresden figurines, pale with an arrogant Nordic grace, and Nikki's heart sank to the bottom of her shoes.

Gordon's male beauty she had expected, but the other one, ah, the other woman was the exact antithesis of Nikki, who was small, and dark, and *scruffy*. As she climbed reluctantly out of the car and saw the cool, disdainful amusement in the other woman's eyes, Nikki thought again of the peacock-blue dress with deepest regret, for she had intended on wearing it for all the soft, seductive reasons of a woman dressing for a man, and she knew now that she would wear it as a declaration of war.

CHAPTER SEVEN

GORDON sauntered over to where Nikki stood, dirty and despairing and squirming internally, and the handsome doctor's face was lit from inside with a beatific joy. 'My love, you are, as always sublime,' he greeted her softly as he took both her hands in his. 'I was so glad to learn from Harper that your hands are almost healed.'

Her teeth set on edge as she smiled up at him, and she gritted very privately, 'I'm a wreck and we both know it, so don't rub it in.'

'Oh, God,' whispered the blond laughing man, 'a woman's vanity. Put it out of your head, my little dearest. Concentrate instead on all the speed limits Harper must have broken to get back home by six o'clock, only to find that nobody was home anxiously awaiting him. Today must have been the first day in fifteen years that he knocked off work early.'

The colour in her sun-kissed cheeks drained away, leaving her looking very pale, with the edge of self-consciousness stripped from those great eyes as they clung to him. 'Are you being serious?' she said, almost begging as her pride blew away on the wind and she focused on Gordon fully for the first time.

'I'll make you one promise, darling,' he said, his blond head bent to hers, 'I'll never lie to you. But we can put it to the test, if you like. Give us a kiss.'

As abruptly as the colour had left her cheeks, it now flooded back in a dark tide. 'Gordon!' she exclaimed in frantic mortification. All too suddenly she became aware of Harper's narrowed, hard stare, of the other woman's raised eyebrows, and, realising how intimate the two of them must look, she pulled away in some confusion from the gleeful doctor.

Charles had already disappeared into the house, leaving the front door swinging open on its hinges, and, anxious to escape before her composure shredded any further, Nikki managed a tight smile as she excused herself. 'Forgive me for rushing away, but I'm dying for a bath.'

'Yes, I dare say,' murmured Gayle, falsely sympathetic while her gaze shot daggered antipathy.

My God, how did I make an enemy of her so quickly? thought Nikki in some dismay. Harper reached into the back of his car, pulled out an overnight case and the large bag of art supplies they had just bought, and said pleasantly, 'Gordon, Gayle, you know your usual rooms. Anne tells me that supper can be served at eight, if that's all right with everyone, so drinks will be at seven-thirty. I'll be going up now, myself.'

He waited and glanced at Nikki with eyebrows slightly raised, and one part of her mind registered the fact that Harper had just pulled one of his favourite tricks again, manipulating a scenario with an adroit master touch, then stepping back to see how everyone reacted. She could walk up the stairs with him now, or somehow manoeuvre to avoid the implications of such companionship, and both Gordon and Gayle were watching to see what she would do.

In another mood, she might have behaved quite differently, but in the complicated unspoken nuances resounding throughout the fresh early evening air she gravitated instinctively towards her most established ally, falling into step beside Harper as naturally as if they had

ascended the stairs together many a time. In response
he gave her a remarkably sweet smile.

'I am sorry about the ice-cream on your suit,' she said
as they entered the house and she began to trudge up
the stairs with a weary sigh. It had been a long, busy
day, and every muscle in her body seemed to be aching.

'I've told you already, it's unimportant.' Harper sent
an oblique glance at her downbent head beside him, and
he asked coolly, 'What did Gordon have to say to you
just now?'

'Gordon?' she replied blankly, slow to catch on. Then
another dark, revealing flush swept over her traitorous
face, leaving her looking as guilty as if she had been
caught in the act of some major sin. Her blue eyes flew
up to his, then very quickly away. 'Oh, that—it was
nothing,' she muttered.

'That "nothing" certainly provoked a most intriguing
reaction,' he murmured with taunting silkiness as they
came up to her bedroom door. When she would have
opened it, he laid aside his case and the shopping basket
and stepped in front of her with a deceptively lazy
movement. She backed against the wall and found herself
trapped as he planted his hands on either side of her
head. 'What's the matter, Nikki—afraid to tell?'

She had gravitated towards her most established ally?
That was a joke. What had got into him, anyway? Where
was the close, gentle camaraderie they had shared in the
art shop only a half an hour ago? Feeling hassled and
flustered, she raised her tousled head and said pointedly,
'I told you, it was unimportant. If you're so concerned
about it, why don't you ask Gordon?'

'Now, there's a thought,' he murmured, and smiled
in a way she didn't trust, for it lit an unpredictable light

in his dark, intent eyes. 'And what would he tell me if I did?'

'Why, to mind your own business, of course,' she remarked lightly, with an ironic quirk of her eyebrows. She was very thankful that he could not climb inside her head and read what was there, for she might have lost her heart to this man, foolishly, precipitately, but she wasn't about to admit to it. It was too soon, too revealing, her chaotic emotions straining against common sense, her desires reined in by insecurity.

He laughed softly to himself, a strange, almost angry kind of sound that sharpened her interest to the point of worry, but she could not imagine what had prompted it. But just as she was opening her mouth to ask him, just as his gaze had dropped to watch the movement of her lips, Charles came galloping around the corner of the hall.

'Harper, see the picture of a spaceship I made for you?'

The inexplicable tense mood that had built up between them disintegrated. Harper stepped away from her unhurriedly, his attention shifting away, and Nikki felt as if she had just escaped from a hot spotlight. She took the opportunity to escape into her room, and leaned weakly against the closed door as she listened to the fading sounds of his deep voice intermingled with the boy's high treble.

Now, what had all that been about? She shook her head over the vagaries of men and went to stare at herself in her mirror. How horrifying—not only did her blouse carry strawberry stains, but the elbows were smudged with pencil marks, and her short black hair stood up in rumpled peaks where she had run her fingers through it distractedly.

She folded her lips into a grim line. No wonder Gayle Chancellor had looked down that perfect aquiline nose at her! She looked like a filthy street urchin. Well, there was nowhere else to go from the bottom but up. She stalked into the bathroom and began an assault on her offending appearance.

After washing her hands with care, quickly so that the healing cuts did not soften too much in the warm water, she pulled on another pair of tight surgical gloves that the local doctor had given her for protection, and ran herself a deep bath. There she wallowed, shampooing her hair and soaping herself until her skin was flushed a bright clean pink.

Then she prepared for the dinner ahead, reassessing every part of what she'd planned on wearing that evening: the very plain but exquisitely crafted pumps, the sheer black tights, the vivid dress that was little more than a silken slip that ended three inches above her slim knees and complemented her blue eyes perfectly and seemed to reflect a raven-black sheen on to the sleek cap of her hair. The dress lay against her skin, all the shape lent to it from her firm, slim body.

She gave an approving nod. It was smart enough and would look even more trendy against any muted elegance she suspected that Gayle would produce.

But the white of her shoulders and arms was broken only by the two thin straps of the dress. Nikki's hand reached for the matching costume jewellery she had bought, and hesitated as she stared at herself with a little private smile. Really, her neck was quite shockingly bare without it.

She abandoned the jewellery and made up her face, and if the young woman in her was unsure about how much eyeshadow and blusher to apply, the artist was in no doubt whatsoever.

She was a little late as she descended the stairs, and heard voices coming from the front reception-room. One part of her was fiercely, jealously glad, for the rear lounge was the intimate scene of Harper's private relaxation that he had shared with her. No matter if the others had been in the room at some other time; Nikki didn't want the memory of her first firelit evening in his house tarnished.

She walked into the front room. Charles was absent, for he was already eating supper in the kitchen, but the other three adults were present. Gordon, restless as always, was by the front window, and his face lit up with pure wicked pleasure when he saw her.

Gayle was sitting gracefully at one end of the couch, her expression wooden, her beautiful eyes filling with fury. For a moment Nikki didn't understand, for they were a perfect foil for each other, the one tall, blonde, coolly elegant in black, the other slight, very dark and vivid with colour. But then she realised that after seeing the grubby woman outside Gayle had been totally unprepared to meet this sleek, dashing image, and Nikki's confidence soared.

Then Harper turned around, saw her, and both the person she admired in him and the friend she was coming to trust were totally subjugated by the virile ascendacy of the rampant male. Their gazes met and clashed with such intensity that she felt the steadiness in her limbs fizzle out. Then, as if he couldn't help it, his dark, ignited eyes lowered but he didn't look away. She knew what he saw, and her breathing grew wildly erratic. He saw what she had wanted him to see—the shape of her unadorned body, the cream of her revealed flesh.

Gordon came around the end of the couch with the grace of a brilliant kingfisher, reached for her hands and brought them to his twitching lips. 'What an astounding transformation!' he exclaimed. 'Darling, you look exquisite!'

Nikki's gaze was late in pulling away from Harper's face, when the doctor leaned forward and whispered into her ear, 'And good enough to eat!'

She trembled at the darkened expression that swept over Harper's hard, forceful features, and she turned to Gordon with the whispered, desperate plea, 'For pity's sake, cut it out!'

'But we've only just begun, you and I,' murmured the blond man, his keen gaze reckless on her delicate, flustered face.

'How dare you?' she breathed in wonder, too shaken for outrage.

'I am playing with fire, aren't I?' replied Gordon with a quicksilver grin. 'God knows, Harper is dangerous when provoked! But my God, this is worth it! Did you ever think that the attentions of another man just might break down this obsessive distance he persists in putting between himself and the rest of the world?'

Her eyes widened in amazement. 'But how did you know of that?'

'My dear, I've seen it from the very beginning. I've watched him grow up, and away from almost everyone around him, and if you can be the one to bring him back to himself you have my sincerest blessing.' Gordon managed to add, in a low mutter, 'I've never seen him look like that! Don't crack under the pressure, darling Nikki!'

'But—but——' she stuttered, hardly knowing how to act, and then Harper was upon them, furious and predatory, and looking for blood. She turned heavy, apprehensive eyes slowly up to him as he stood in front of them, exuding sultry menace, and was shocked to discover that there was nothing of it in his expression, nothing but urbane politeness. Harper was the total image of the civilised man, but his eyes were primeval.

'Perrier, Nikki?' he asked velvetly as he held a glass out to her.

Even as she reached for it, a thanks ready to be murmured from her lips, Gordon exclaimed, 'Perrier? Surely you'd like something stronger than that, my dear?'

She caught her breath, frightened and stunned at the way Harper turned to his friend—such a simple movement of the body, just an economic twist from that taut male waist that had all the quality of a snarling wolf rounding on its enemy. She couldn't believe how Gordon had the courage to face it, even as Harper said very quietly, 'Nikki never drinks anything but a glass of wine with supper.'

Gordon's eyebrows lifted audaciously. 'Is Nikki ever given a choice?'

Harper smiled, white and gentle, and at the sight the fearful tension exploded out of her with the exclamation, 'For God's sake! It's Nikki's choice that she never has anything but one glass of wine, and she also hates being discussed as if she weren't here!'

The blond man turned to her with a tender, flirtatious expression. 'Believe me, darling, I'm all too aware of your presence in that incredible dress!'

As Harper's dark eyes plummeted into savagery, Gayle said from behind Gordon's shoulder, her flinty voice striking sparks, 'Is this a private fight, or can anyone join in?'

Oh, dear heaven, thought Nikki in despair, how bad can this get? Already the evening was a smoking débâcle.

It got, in fact, much worse. Most of the hostilities went underground. Throughout supper Gordon behaved incorrigibly like a man smitten with desire; only the laughter throbbing in his low voice as he whispered to Nikki gave him away. Torn between the hard, ruthless contemplation of every change in Nikki's volatile expression, and his duties as host, Harper conversed with Gayle as his gaze grew more and more violent.

And the other woman, Nikki saw, was narrowly watching the entire interplay, her haughty, inscrutable face revealing none of her thoughts.

Gordon gave her an unsympathetic explanation during one of his whispered exchanges. 'Gayle's always had one eye on her chances with Harper, but don't worry, nothing's ever come of it. And, fool that I am, I've chased after her for years while she's blown hot and cold on me. So refreshing to give her a taste of her own medicine. At the moment she looks absolutely frigid, doesn't she?' he concluded with a certain callous admiration.

'I don't blame her!' replied Nikki from between gritted teeth, disappointed at not being able to enjoy the superb meal as the others seemed to have done.

From the head of the table, as he lounged back in his seat, Harper asked lazily, 'Who don't you blame, Nikki?'

Her cowardly gaze had barely collided with his before bouncing away, and, suddenly so sick of the fulminating atmosphere, she resorted to her innate core of honesty and snapped, 'I don't blame Gayle, of course, if she never wanted to speak to Gordon again! He's behaving abominably, and if this supper's any indication of what's to follow, thank you very much, but I'll skip dessert!'

The two men burst out laughing, and she sat frozen, frantically willing herself not to blush, for of course even as the words left her mouth she realised that she had shot them all back to the very first night they had met, and what she had said about Gordon's interrupted tête-à-tête.

Only Gayle was in the dark about the joke, and to Nikki's intense relief neither man chose to enlighten her. The blonde woman didn't seem to notice the lack, however, her well-bred expression filling with surprise as she stared at Nikki.

Pride won out; she managed not to colour, and by her frankness and a miracle of timing an undeclared cease-fire seemed to be a unanimous conclusion as the mood of the room lightened considerably. Even Gayle's hostility became less overt as she addressed Nikki in conversation for the first time with a hint of civility, though the sharp calculation in her eyes never dissipated. Nikki was so relieved tensions had eased that she didn't even mind that they moved into the rear lounge for coffee and liqueurs.

Harper poured the coffee himself, which was already waiting on a Victorian mahogany table inlaid with gold and ivory. He handed cups to Gayle and Gordon first, then brought Nikki's over to her. She took the china saucer carefully, and murmured a subdued thanks with her gaze downcast. Watching that her coffee didn't spill wasn't an excuse. She was so disturbed by the odd, relentless way Harper had moved towards her that her fingers were dangerously unsteady.

He did not go back to retrieve a cup for himself. Instead he stood in front of her as she hovered near the French doors, which were open to the warm, dark evening. Nikki turned her head and stared out to the night, wishing with all her frenetic heart that she could escape from this intolerable situation.

'Look at me,' said Harper softly.

She shook her head as if in negation, resignation, then threw it back and raised her gaze to his face, drawn like a helpless moth into the dark flames of his eyes. She was dumbfounded. How could she have convinced herself that all the lowering tension had dissipated? Relations had eased, politeness restored, but Harper still contained in his tight, strong body the powder keg that Gordon had lit with a match.

The china cup in the saucer she held rattled audibly. Without taking his ferocious stare away from hers, Harper reached out and wrapped one hand around her wrist. It steadied her and shackled her, his hot, calloused palm rasping along her sensitive skin.

'Of course, you know how close I came to losing control this evening,' said Harper pleasantly. God, but he was *furious*.

She set her teeth, breathing in short, shallow pants. 'I had no part in the game Gordon was playing,' she told him, and was inordinately proud at achieving an edged calm.

'Don't you think I'm aware of that?' His taut mouth, shaping the sharp words, held a smouldering fascination for her. She stared, unable to look away, as a sweet, burning liquid weakened the muscles of her body and threatened to drown her. 'I know how you don't like to play mind games, but my God, if you had encouraged him, I think I could have killed you both!'

Anger fused incandescently inside her, born of passion and outrage. Her eyes flared up, locked with him, and she whispered, 'What a convenient, useless warning since you and I both know that it can't change the inevitable!'

Harper's breath whistled in a sibilant hiss, and he looked as if he could have struck her. He gritted, 'You take too much for granted!'

'I have taken nothing except a chance!' she flashed. 'I dressed this way, tonight, for you, but I have no power over your reaction and I cannot help it if other men might be attracted by what they see! And if you refuse to take what's offered, you have no right to prevent someone else! That is what's inevitable, and I am not sorry your pride is offended by the thought that you might have to compete for something for once in your life!'

Still he fought it, trying desperately to clamp restraint on the marauding fury that devastated all reason and consideration, and her eyes widened with a sudden, stricken sense of understanding. She knew now why she had entertained so many doubts about Harper at first, and it wasn't wholly because of her past experiences.

The two sides of Harper's personality—his aggressive ruthlessness and his gentle patience—were essentially incompatible, eternally straining at one another. If he was filled with rage that evening, most was turned against himself for his primitive and uncontrolled reaction that evening. Now the two sides were being pulled apart in living torment.

'You don't know what you're asking of me!' he grated out, half gasped, averting his harsh-boned face in rejection.

But, oh, now she did, and despair crushed down on her. Her eyes and face filled with it as she acknowledged defeat and stepped back from the conflict. She said quietly, even gently, 'I know that by trying to protect me from yourself you have protected me too well.'

She had no desire to prolong this terrible evening. She turned away from Harper, whose hand fell nerveless to his side, and carefully set down the coffee she had not drunk. Both Gordon and Gayle, having settled in quiet conversation at the other end of the room, looked at her strained, set face in sharp curiosity.

She gave them a brittle little smile and said simply, 'It's late and I'm tired, so I'll say goodnight now.'

They echoed the goodnight, the other woman cool and reserved, Gordon with a slight edge of concern. Nikki couldn't bear to look at Harper as she exited the room without fuss, but the other two did. All they saw, however, was a blank, unrevealing statue.

The hot tears came as she climbed up the stairs, not in a weak cascade but slow and hard. She had seen it; from the very beginning she had seen it, but had not understood. Harper's passion was bound up inextricably with his ruthlessness, his driving ambition, all the powerful, dynamic emotions that were pitted against the gentler side of the man. He could not separate them and he would not offer her the dangerous side; whenever they had broken down the barriers between them in shrieking fury and desire he had always built back the restraints, just as he had kissed her so explosively last Sunday and yet had managed to walk away.

Well, this time Nikki had walked away. This time she was the one to look on him in grief and pity and say, 'No more'. She did not need to know if she had the power to break down that resistance of his. Everything inside her would only mourn the destructiveness. She longed, pined, ached, needed for him to come to her of his own free will, and had to come to bitter terms with the realisation that he would not.

She entered her empty, dark room, which seemed so hot and airless that she crossed over to her balcony door to throw it open. The fresh, cool breeze was like a shock of icy water thrown in her face, and she wrapped her arms around her body with a shivering sob. Maybe Harper was big enough, mature enough, wise enough to be able to offer her only the gentle side in friendship, but she didn't think she was big enough to take it. And she didn't think she could live without it.

She turned her thoughts to the desolate consideration of leaving Oxford. It had to come sooner or later. She had proved not only that her hands were healed enough for survival, but that now they could work again. Nikki turned away from the open door and wandered through her shadowed room at random. She couldn't leave tomorrow, for it seemed somehow too rude to break up the weekend, but she could ask Harper for a ride back to London on Sunday night. But what about Charles? How could she say goodbye to those trusting dark eyes, that clever little face?

Misjudging the placement of the furniture, she blundered into the side of the wardrobe and just leant there, turning her face into the corner by the wall.

'You need,' said Harper in a quiet voice from the balcony, 'someone with a great deal more kindness than I could give you.'

Both shock and pain flayed at already raw nerves. He couldn't have hurt her more if he had deliberately tried. She gasped, her streaked face sliding along the wall, and snarled, 'Get out!'

But both footsteps and voice sounded closer. Harper walked around the corner of the bed. 'You need someone who won't interfere with your career, who won't be so jealous of that all-consuming absorption that drives everything else out of your mind when you work.'

'God damn you!' she sobbed in anguish, and shoved the white knuckles of one hand against her distorted

mouth. How much more completely could he reject her?
She didn't know, but this was destroying her.

He was almost behind her. He was—— Two hands
like thunderbolts descended on to her quaking shoulders,
and turned her roughly so that the room spun and her
breath left her in a soundless gasp. 'You need someone
with the strength of character to take your innocence
patiently,' he groaned, and a ragged shiver rippled
through his body. 'Oh, Nikki, help me!'

She broke and cried it out loud. 'I need you!'

He hauled her into his arms, driving his mouth down
hard over hers. She could feel the imprint of his teeth
behind his lips the instant before they opened and savaged
hers apart; he moved one big hand behind her head and
compulsively drove his tongue into her like a spear.

She erupted into white heat. She was in an agony she
could not end, wrapping her arms around his neck,
piercing herself on his mouth, his body, his hands. The
sound that shuddered from him was animalistic; he arced
his head back with a gasp as she plunged her fingers into
the satin pelt of his hair.

He reached down over her hips to grasp her dress and
pull it up, and she was so far gone into the mating ur-
gency that she didn't even comprehend the meaning of
the sound as it ripped. His mouth had left hers to travel
unsteadily along her cheek, his rough voice a furnace
blast on flinching skin. 'You could grow to hate me for
this.'

'You fool!' she groaned, as his fingers connected with
the bare skin of her waist and jerked uncontrollably at
the erotic contact. She tried to get at the buttons of his
shirt, but they were too close together and her hands
shook too much. She nearly cried in frustration and in-

stead bent hungrily to lick at his neck, stunned by his unique taste of human salt.

'God!' He writhed as if in pain and yanked her head away, and though her lips formed a puzzled, anxious query she never got to ask it as he took her mouth in primitive, unassuaging appetite over and over again.

She was as helpless as a dandelion puff in a howling storm of sensation. When she felt the slow but unmistakable indications of his withdrawal, she leaned weakly against the wall behind her and made a faint, uncomprehending sound of hurt. He couldn't. He couldn't do this to her again and just leave.

He gave her a swift kiss. 'Shh, darling,' he whispered hoarsely, a large, dark presence that moved and shrugged to the sigh of clothing being discarded.

She couldn't have been more tipsy had she been stark raving drunk, and without his support she slid down the wall until she was in a crumpled heap at his feet. Her ripped dress had slid back down into place; she yanked it off and threw it away just as his shirt billowed down over her head. Nikki wrapped her arms around it and greedily crushed the warm, scented material to her face.

Above her sounded an unsteady laugh. 'Where the hell did you go?'

'Here,' she murmured dreamily, lifting her arms towards him like a child as he bent, slid his arms underneath her and picked her up. Both of them reacted audibly to the electric contact of bare, hard flesh to flesh. She shuddered as his whole wide chest rippled and flexed when he strode towards her bed and laid her down gently.

He ran those long hands over her body, sliding calloused fingers over the bare tips of her nipples, along the slim ribcage now thudding wildly, and with an ef-

fortless whisper of frictional silk he stripped away her
tights and she was naked.

Then he came down on top of her, hard and hot and
heavy, and he grew to know her with his lips and his
hands, every inch of her body. He suckled at her breasts
and rubbed the moistened nipples with the balls of his
thumbs, purring deep in his throat when she cried out
at the unbearable sensitisation. He taught her all the
pleasure points with exquisite, unrelenting tenderness that
levelled her inside, then built her up to a suspense which
only he understood, only he could see to conclusion.

Then he gently parted her legs, and brought forth an
explosion of flowering, moist pleasure where before there
had been only a desert, until at last she jerked and sobbed
out, 'Stop—stop now!'

Harper smiled into the darkness, turned his face into
the quivering muscles of her soft, vulnerable stomach
and whispered, 'No.'

God, she was in torment. It was too much pleasure,
too much love she felt for this hard, gentle, fiercely voluptuous man, and her tortured breath dragged in a
thickened throat, and she tried to scream, but it came
out in a reedy, urgent gasp. 'I can't take this!'

'Oh, yes, you can,' he told her melodiously, only she
was dying from it, but then her body convulsed, and
rippled, and shook so that she thought she would never
stop, and he rose from lying alongside her to come between her innocent legs and meet with that gossamer
barrier, taking it from her forever.

She groaned, a long, descending note, at the incredible experience, and, misunderstanding, he stroked
the sides of her damp face with his big hands and whispered raggedly, 'Shush, shush, it's gone.'

How strange he sounded, almost grieving, as if he would take her pain along with everything else, and her arms tightened fiercely around him as she echoed on an incredulous gasp, 'Gone? Ah, Harper, it was nothing compared to this!'

His body moved in a silent exhalation of air as her words drove into him like shimmering arrows, and he lay with his head beside hers in supplication as he moved and moved with the force of a tidal wave, ascending, racing, arcing, diving down until he broke in her, the wave crashing upon an unknown shore.

Nikki was in a warm cave that moved when she moved, moulding itself to the contours of her body, and she sighed as she burrowed, sleeping, lulled by an ever-present rhythm thrumming in her ear. Her whole body was suffused with comfort and well-being, her awakening languorous as she turned under the heavy bed-covers, seeking her hard pillow of shoulder, the arm that had welcomed her all night and cradled her against him——

She bolted into sharp awareness, remembering last night even as she discovered Harper's absence, a sweet echo of fulfilment, a numbing sense of loss.

She was alone in her bed, the room cold with fresh early morning air streaming through the open balcony door. The pillow beside hers still had the imprint from where Harper had lain, spiced with his scent, and she dragged it down to stuff it against her abdomen, curling around it to ease the empty ache.

It seemed that once she had embarked on the sensual exploration there was no stopping. What was the proper etiquette for the morning after lovemaking? she wondered miserably. Should she now be feeling so abandoned and forlorn? She was in love with him, so hopelessly, inextricably tangled into emotional and physical love, and she knew she couldn't pretend to light-hearted affection when next she saw him; she could only, helplessly, be herself, and it felt like failure.

A shadow fell across the doorway, and her black head lifted. Harper checked when he saw her. 'Oh—you're awake already,' he said, his face breaking into a delighted smile. 'I was only gone five minutes. I went to get my robe and some wood from the bin in my room—yours isn't stocked. This bedroom's so seldom occupied, the fireplace isn't used much. Are you cold, darling?'

Nikki shook her head as she cleared her throat, sinking deep into the bed until only her great blue eyes peered at him over the edge. Her heart stirred with tenderness and passion at the sight of him, grey hair tousled, the change in his face remarkable from the stress-stern visage from yesterday. His shoulders were broad under the casually belted terry robe, a dark sheen of sprinkled hair across the taut muscled chest. Yesterday he had looked impassive, stamped with authority and hard-angled; today he was the version of a younger man, and he was beautiful.

I love you, she almost said, but she held it at the back of her teeth, for even she knew that they were in the full, palest flush of new sharing which had yet to face the rigours and trials of real life, and she was too afraid.

He set the fire, lit it and as it began to pop and hiss in the hearth he straightened from his crouch in one lithe upsurge, quickly moving to shut the balcony door as he slanted his quick dark gaze over one shoulder. 'What's wrong?'

Her uncertain blue eyes widened, but she answered with some spirit, 'Did I say anything was?'

'Did you have to?' he returned, coming back to the bed, so overwhelming to face in the light of day as he casually threw back the covers and draped his long form beside her.

She could never resist him. Even as he reached for her she was melting towards the embrace, and she buried her face into his chest where the bathrobe parted, muttering, 'It's so stupid.'

He ran his hands down her bare back, dark gaze following the path of his fingers along the curves and hollows of her pale skin, and his voice was very soft. 'Tell me anyway.'

'Well,' she said simply, muffled against him, 'I woke up and you weren't here.'

He made a crooning sound of compassion, turned her over and kissed her softly, but somewhere in the middle of it the tempo changed, heightened, deepened, and drugged them both. At last he pulled away and fell back on the pillows, while Nikki objected to the withdrawal symptoms and came after him.

Harper lay at peace, face upturned, profile etched by the early morning light. She curled around his shoulder, looking her fill, and other than his hand wandering idly along the curve of her hip he remained passive. She ran her fingers over his face, not very gently, feeling the straight rivulets marking the sides of his eyes and mouth. He sighed, dark eyes hooding, and lifted his face to the touch; and she fastened on to the hair at his strong nape, leaned over and brought her lips down on his to invade him as hungrily as he had invaded her last night, and his arm fastened around her hips like an iron vice.

They collided in each other's mouth as if they were fighting a duel, and she leaned on his chest and on her forearms, running her fingers down to span the width of his columned neck. He reached and lifted her right off the bed at the waist, and she gasped at how effortlessly he did it, and he brought her over him until she straddled his torso, all the time watching her face as it flooded with surprise and comprehension, his hooded eyes gone erotically ferocious.

He grasped her by the hips, and held her, great, strong arms locked rigid and steady, until she felt the pressure of being suspended without release over his supple, aroused body. She curved over him as if in pain, reaching for him, guiding him with clumsy, untutored hands, and the look in his eyes was like nothing she had ever seen before: tender and ruthless and insatiable.

He arced his body, thrusting into her, vast and swift, and subsided, still holding her aloft as she cried out a hoarse, clawing frustration. Then he smiled and she saw it, and he brought her down, impaling her, and his face was transformed with triumph and exquisite agony.

All the while the bright little fire crackled merrily in the hearth, like the sound of crumpled wrapping paper at Christmas.

CHAPTER EIGHT

THEY breakfasted later with the others. Charles had scampered down quite early, looking clean and bright-eyed and deceptively cherubic, and over golden waffles topped with strawberries and cream he proceeded to regale Gordon with the newest of his acquired jokes.

Harper had been extremely solicitous to her sensibilities, Nikki reflected, as the fresh tangy fruit and crispy waffle burst a luscious combination of tastes in her mouth. He had showered while she huddled under her bedcovers, sensually replete and wide-eyed with a kind of naïve amazement at what had happened to her over the last night. Then he had kissed her briefly, told her he was going to dress and go downstairs, and that she should come down only when she was ready to.

After he had left she couldn't stay in bed for long, and had washed and dressed hurriedly, impatient for the day to start and eager to snatch as much precious time with Harper as she could. Dressing indifferently in dungarees and an oversized striped shirt, she skipped down the stairs with a light step while running her fingers through her short hair to comb it. She succeeded only in making it stand up in raven peaks at her forehead, and wouldn't have cared had she known.

When she reached the dining-room she stopped, poised on one foot as she hovered intensely at the doorway, her impetuous gaze sweeping over the room and alighting on Harper, who lounged indolently in one chair, a cup of coffee in front of him as he chatted to a cool, elegant Gayle.

For a terrible moment all the old uncertainty had rushed back, and Nikki was left standing with her mind a blank, not knowing what to do or say or even how to feel, until Harper caught sight of her out of the corner of his eye and turned his head.

It had all been there in his eyes—the profound pleasure at her appearance, amused, conspiratorial delight, and a certain measure of gentle resignation, and understanding had blossomed in her in a split instant. It was up to her how public she chose to make their relationship, and if she said nothing he would say nothing.

Nikki's whole face came to glorious life, and she shook her head a little at him as if in despair over his incredible obtuseness, to which Harper laughed out loud, his stern face singularly altered. Gayle, sitting to one side of the table in a casual khaki skirt and light green top, stared incredulously at Harper as if she had never seen him before, then turned to stare at Nikki.

All the unmistakable signs were there: the bruised peach of her lips, the deep pallor of sleeplessness to her translucent skin, the delicate bluish hollows around her luminous, dazzling eyes. She looked exactly as she felt— exhausted and radiant after a night of lovemaking.

Nikki had seen the stiff shock that froze Gayle's features. There, the whole thing's as good as public now without ever an exchange of words, she thought, and all she felt was a tremendous relief. She wouldn't pretend, not now or ever, but even as she tensed to hurtle towards Harper, who had held out an inviting, peremptory hand, she hesitated and watched his confident smile slip a notch.

Ah, it was some deeper instinct than she'd known she had that made her give him a tight, wicked grin that challenged and teased and mocked, and she whirled lightly on her feet in flamboyant rejection as she went to pour herself a coffee from the hot urn on the sideboard.

Only Gayle saw Harper's expression. He still laughed, but it was a roused, hard laughter, the dark eyes wolfish, that smiling mouth ruthless. The blonde woman shuddered in convulsive reaction, and she wondered if the younger girl knew what she was doing.

No one was witness to Gayle's expression: her glittering overlay of ice in her eyes, sharp to a cutting edge, the perfect features frozen in a winter of the soul.

After some discussion over breakfast they decided to go to a charity fête being given at the grounds of a local hospital. Harper would drive the Jaguar, in which everyone would fit, and while the general assumption was that Nikki would take the front seat she adroitly skipped around that and gave up the position to Gayle. Her heart was not in control under Harper's very sharp, watchful gaze; it thudded wildly to a beat of his devising and it took all her strength of will to combat the effect and retain a mind of her own.

Nikki knew that she was playing with fire just as Gordon had last night, and of all the others she thought she caught a glimmer of sympathetic understanding in the handsome doctor's eyes. Gordon had been the one, after all, to give her the vital clue. Harper was hers only for now, and he might not be in the future. She did not think he loved her yet, and she wanted desperately for him to, but she had to hide that very desperation.

She knew she couldn't afford to let him be too gentle, for it would be the eventual death knell of their relationship. Not only was Harper's gentler, wiser side the source of his restraint, but his ruthless, ambitious side had to be satisfied, or passion would die and he would wander away.

To keep him she had to be the eternal conquest, she realised with a deep shiver. He was too complex. If he had wished for either a refined, civilised wife, or a totally professional partner, he would have married by now, but Harper needed a combination of both passion and challenge, and it would take every ounce of her independent, intuitive personality to live up to that.

When Gordon, Charles and Nikki had arranged themselves in the back, she was behind the driver's seat and had to sustain a particularly barbarous spear thrown from Harper's hard glance as he slammed her door and slid behind the wheel.

Part of her was in a state of shock. She couldn't conceive of how such satisfying lovemaking could feed her hunger, not assuage it, and her nostrils quivered in tremulous reaction as she caught the faintest ephemeral whiff of his scent. She couldn't help herself and leaned forward against the back of his seat, her head ostensibly turned to Gordon, who sat talking at the opposite rear door, on the other side of Charles.

Nikki slid her hand stealthily between the driver's seat and the door, and her fingers collided with Harper's torso. She felt but did not hear his sharp intake of breath and, unseen by any of them, she stroked him from breast muscle to that athletic waist, while he sat rigid and unmoving.

Suddenly her lips parted in a silent gasp as he captured her wandering hand and crushed it roughly against the hard bone of his hip. Her fingers, slim and helpless under pressure of his, throbbed. Some sixth sense lifted her head. Harper was looking at her in the rear-view mirror, amused and aroused and savage. She was caught like a rabbit in the hypnotic effect, unaware that she licked her lips, until she saw his gaze fall to the tiny voluptuous movement.

The entire exchange lasted barely a moment, just long enough for Gordon to finish whatever it was he had been saying and for Gayle to give a quick reply, and for Charles to twist in his seat and grow restless. 'Aren't we ready yet?' snapped the boy impatiently.

'Sorry,' drawled Harper lazily as he gave her fingers a painful admonitory pinch, 'I was just wool-gathering.'

'Oh, very bland,' Nikki said in an approving tone before she could help herself, and she earned the reflection of a white volcanic smile.

He advised her softly, 'Sit back and behave yourself.'

Laughing and shaken, she did just that while Charles and Gordon glanced at them in puzzlement, aware that what they had seen was scorching and private, and, to them, incomprehensible.

Nikki's attention went to Gayle. The other woman's gaze was inscrutable and piercing; before she had written Nikki off, then been angered at that underestimation. Now Nikki would have sworn that she was being probed in some manner, and it made her uneasy to see such intent without knowing the reason behind it.

The fête was large and very crowded, and it took them a long time to weave their way around the various stalls. All the while that searing, spitting undercurrent raced between Harper and Nikki and manifested itself in the growl of his voice, the snap in her bright eyes.

They had tea and sandwiches at one of the tents, managing to claim an empty table to one side. Charles had yet more strawberries and cream, while Nikki succumbed to the extravagance of a chocolate eclair. She consumed the pastry with a delighted greed that brought an indulgent smile to Gordon's face and derisive amusement to Gayle's. She saw it and shrugged; she didn't care, she was enjoying herself. What baffled her was when she quickly glanced sideways at Harper and found in his dark eyes an eruptive, ravenous expression that threatened to shake her body apart.

When she was finished, he reached out with one slow hand, cupped her chin, and turned her face to him. Puzzled, Nikki complied with the gesture, and as she looked swimmingly into his intent gaze he ran his forefinger down the corner of her lips in a delicate caress, captured a speck of cream and chocolate and showed it to her. She coloured a little, laughing silently at herself, and then all the laughter died away as he put the finger to his mouth and licked it sensuously while watching her.

The hectic blush across her cheekbones deepened until she was feverishly hot. She was burning up from the inside, and he had hardly even touched her. Her shattered gaze wavered and fell, to the accompaniment of his quiet, purring chuckle. My God, she thought dazedly, this is some kind of war of seduction and Harper's holding all the trump cards.

It excited and threatened her, for she felt gloriously intoxicated, dangerously out of control; once again he was reading her like a book, and she felt that his triumph was coming too easily to him and he would get bored with her all the sooner.

She accorded him a major victory and fled in full rout, playing the only trump in her possession as she disconnected and played her mental game with the other people around her. Charles was getting impatient with the crowd and would ask to go home soon. Gayle would be quick to agree, for the older woman was wearing her 'frigid' expression that drove Gordon to such excesses.

She had read the atmosphere right, and soon they were heading back to the house, while Gordon began to chip away at Gayle's composure, Charles thought he monopolised Harper's attention with a rambling soliloquy on everything that the cats and dogs had done that week, and Nikki stared thoughtfully out of the car window. When they arrived back Charles got banished to his room for ignoring several pointed suggestions to change the subject and behave more sociably, and in the general dispersement Nikki wandered down the hall towards the rear lounge.

She had so much to think about, and so much to decide. She knew she had fallen in love with Harper too soon, and she had to school herself to patience as she waited to see whether he would fall in love with her or not. But the trouble was, how long would she have to wait? Months, years, forever?

She fought the impetuous panic that thought produced, for she could not comprehend living with this uncertainty, this insecurity indefinitely. Six months, she thought, suddenly remembering the painting she had agreed to do for Harper. I can cope with the thought of six months, yet a lot can happen in that time. After that, who knows? She didn't have to worry about it now, did she? In the meantime, what about London?

She heard him before she saw him, the swift run of a big man extraordinarily light on his feet, and she turned to face the doorway as Harper rounded it and swooped on her. All her rational thinking descended into a gibbering breathlessness as her idiotic heartbeat betrayed her again, and her eyes went as wide as a child's.

He caught her up, set her against the wall and pinned her there with his body as his grey-maned head bent over hers. He said vividly, his dark eyes predatory, 'I thought I'd never get you on your own.'

Her head fell back against the wall as desire exploded in her veins, and she murmured, 'So do we have cause for celebration?'

She hardly knew what she said but, whatever it was, it didn't matter; the communication that was all-important pulsed in both his body and hers. However, somewhat to her surprise, Harper took her statement seriously and replied to it, his mouth turning grim. 'That remains to be seen.'

At that cryptic statement her eyebrows furrowed together, but he didn't pause to explain himself. Instead, he grabbed hold of her hand and pivoted on one heel. He was clenched, intense; she could feel the tension vibrating down his arm. He dragged her out of the house and Nikki trotted along beside him obligingly, curious as to what he had in mind and patient enough to wait for the explanation.

That he wanted to show her something was obvious. Several possibilities ran through her mind as he took her to the garage, which was a separate building from the house. Harper withdrew from his pocket a key and unlocked a side-door, which opened to a staircase that he strode up. Nikki followed, and, of all the half-drawn conclusions she had come up with, what she saw at the head of the stairs was completely outside them and took her breath away.

Gavin's mysterious work in the garage over the last week, noticed, shrugged at and half forgotten, was suddenly explained, for visible in the large room was the evidence of recently completed carpentry where walls had been torn down and the markings of where they'd been were plastered over. The floor was bare, one huge skylight set into the roof still had new stickers on it, and in one corner was an empty and waiting easel. There were shelves of art supplies, canvasses and brushes and paints, and Nikki's experienced glance quickly told her that everything was of the highest quality.

Harper had planned this—ages ago, before they were lovers, before she knew she loved him, when? Last weekend? As early as last Friday when he first invited her? This—was a staggering statement of intent that wiped the mind blank; she was appalled, frightened, no, terrified. Was he so sure of her, or was he so arrogant? Either possibility in her mind verged on the unacceptable.

He watched her expressive little face, saw the outrage, the fear, the stiffening incredulity. His own face hardened and he said in a harsh voice, 'I gave Gavin instructions for this on Monday morning, before I left for London.'

'I did wonder,' she muttered tightly from between bloodless lips. She took several steps away from him, pretended to look over the paints, put her hand over her mouth.

'Nikki,' he said then, with extreme care, and it was both revealing and inexplicable, 'you aren't the only one to take a chance.'

Her head tilted back. She pushed the fleshy part of her thumb into her mouth and bit it, thinking back to last night as he had meant her to, and how he had said that she took too much for granted and she had corrected him. Was he saying this was not arrogance? What, then? What, Harper?

'I don't understand,' she whispered at last, her shoulders hunched, still afraid. This was outside what she knew of him, and herself, and was anything really the way she perceived it?

'No, I know,' he said, and the tightness was gone from his voice, replaced by something else. Gentleness, sadness. 'We haven't very much between us, after all. An accidental meeting, very little history.'

She made a sound of pain, didn't know why, bit her thumb all the harder.

'Do you trust me, Nikki?'

How quietly he reached out with the words, without either passion or threat, stabilising all those incoherent, half-completed thoughts of alarm. How quietly he made her consider just that question alone and nothing else. She thought and took her time, for it was so important, even though the answer was obvious.

'Yes,' she said, a thread of sound connecting them together, and she thought she heard him sigh.

'Then, my love——' How delicately he said it, and moved, until his touch came feather-light at the nape of her exposed neck. 'Can you trust me enough not to worry for the moment about why I had this done? I have my reasons, and they are important to me. I will tell you some time, but please, not now. Just consider this a given choice, for yourself and not for me. There's space, privacy, plenty of light and safety, and if you look around you can see that you are welcome. Would you like to work here?'

He asked her not to question his motives, but why? Why? Why? pounded in her brain until she covered her face in distress and confusion. Think, Nikki. Two sides of the man, one dynamic, passionate, powerful, the other gentle and wise and kind. Two sides, incompatible, straining against each other.

She did not think that if she refused this remarkable invitation they would immediately stop seeing each other. Knightsbridge and Mayfair in London were within easy access of each other. But conducting the relationship here in Oxford meant something important to him, perhaps vital; what? London or Oxford, seeing him during the week in the evenings, or seeing him at the weekends?

But there was plenty of light and safety here. His linkage of words, not hers. And there were two sides, power and gentleness, and he wanted her in the gentleness. It was the same old conflict in him and followed a familiar pattern, where next came restraint, and then withdrawal, and then—the end?

So staying was dangerous. But he had his reasons, and the time and the money spent on this new studio were full evidence of that. And he had the vast measure of his maturity and experience, whereas all Nikki had was her instinct.

Well, she could gamble. No matter how he tried to couch this in beneficial terms, he made this invitation for himself, not for her. Her bed-sit in London was fine enough for her. She wanted to know his reasons so she would stay, but it took all her courage to lift her head and turn to face him, to inject hauteur and pride in her face.

'I'll stay,' she said, by her very manner telling him that she was conceding to his wish without gratitude, and she added, with the merest touch of insolence, 'For now.'

And she could have cried as she drove that essential wedge between them, as his lean, handsome face toughened and his eyes lit with dark fire, as they stood face to face and clashed in their attraction and their conflict.

'So you tell me,' Harper said softly, as he reached for her arms and pulled her hard against him, 'do we have cause for celebration?'

Her unshed tears gave her the strength to smile recklessly into his glittering eyes. 'Well, darling,' she drawled, the bite in her words a challenge in itself as she gave his own words back to him, 'that remains to be seen.'

Harper bent his head, a dark flush on his angled, taut cheekbones, his eyes half hooded, the shape of his mouth evocative, terse, exciting as he whispered, 'Kiss on it.'

He took her softened mouth, plundering greedily as once more the sexual wildfire consumed them both, and, if this ardent, knowledgeable lover was not the friend she would have liked to turn to at that moment in her insecurity and need, she knew why she had to meet him in her strength and not in her weakness.

For she could not afford to let him be too gentle.

CHAPTER NINE

ON SUNDAY after breakfast Harper made their excuses to Gordon and Gayle, and strolled with Nikki into the library, where she went to her stack of pencil drawings and shuffled through them nervously.

She told herself that she was being ridiculous, but the inner admonition sounded hollow even to her ears, for a slight but definite change had come over Harper as he entered the room and sat down in a large padded armchair. Gone was the tender, exciting lover of the last two nights, and in his place sat the cool, dispassionate businessman, and she knew that, despite everything they had shared, if her work did not come up to his standards, he would be debilitatingly prompt in telling her so.

Resolutely she shoved aside her self-consciousness and turned to face him, leaning against the wide, heavy table while she called her own professionalism to the fore.

'I've had a look through all the material you left for me,' she said quietly, ducking her dark head as she stared at her drawings with a deep frown. 'And I've come up with two different approaches to the situation. Both are valid for different reasons, so it really comes down to a matter of personal choice. The first set of designs is dynamic and aggressive, and the second has far more of an establishment image, settled, classic, and extremely simple. I—I'm sorry I haven't had time yet to come up with colour sketches. What I have here is pretty rough.'

'Nonsense, you've done well to come up with what you have so quickly,' he replied, holding out a hand for the papers she clutched so tightly. She handed them over and watched his face as he scanned through them unhurriedly. 'What colours did you envisage for these?'

'The same for either design,' she replied. 'I have in mind a heavy cream parchment paper for your stationery—it's expensive, but, I think, well worth the cost. Peter's got samples in his office if you would care to see it. Then either a matt or glossy black lettering, with perhaps a touch of gold. Nothing too fancy, or "arty", as this will date the material, and it's a simple matter of continuing the same design on the quarterly magazine you publish for your clients, so continuity isn't a problem.'

He nodded, then fixed her with a keen, analytical stare. 'You're right, of course. Both are valid choices, but tell me, which do you prefer?'

'Personally?' she said with a smile. 'I like the aggressive one. It's very representative of the immense, wide-reaching success you've achieved worldwide. But I don't necessarily think it is the wisest choice—the people you do business with already know your reputation. They don't need to feel threatened every time they receive a letter or a magazine from you in the post, and they're more likely to be willing to trust and rely on the other image for its aura of stability.'

'A clever assessment,' he remarked as he set the papers aside. 'And I quite agree with you. We'll go with the classic approach.'

She asked anxiously, 'Are those designs all right, or do you want me to see if I can come up with something else?'

Suddenly the businessman vanished, as he gave her a warm smile so filled with pleasure that the strength seeped away from the backs of her knees. 'Darling, they're beautifully thought out, and I love them. And we can carry the design into the offices when we redecorate, so don't you dare change a thing.'

When they left the library, Nikki was glowing, warm with the sincere praise Harper had heaped on her, and from the sensual impact of his mouth caressing hers.

All was right with her world; the day flew past on sun-kissed wings. Gordon got called away on a medical matter, so Gayle would be travelling back to London with Harper. Nikki took a cup of tea into the rear lounge and relaxed by the open windows in the late afternoon, feeling the let-down of the end of the weekend, and struggling to deny how she would miss Harper's presence beside her in bed.

Something, some small noise or psychic instinct, had her head turning. The tender light in her eyes was quickly shuttered as she looked up into Gayle's worldly, cool green eyes.

The older woman, immaculate in a light, tailored linen suit, smiled a little, and it was as frosty and as poised as her appearance. Gayle settled into a nearby chair and laid one arm along the arm of it, resting her chin in elegant fingers.

Nikki averted her face from the critical judgement she saw in Gayle's expression, and said lightly, 'All ready to go?'

'Yes,' replied the blonde languidly, 'we'll be leaving soon. Harper's just calling Duncan to warn him what time we'll be back for supper.'

Nikki's hypersensitive heart missed a beat. They weren't staying for supper here? Harper and Gayle, eating together in his town house, was an image of perfectly matched elegance. She hadn't known that Gayle was one of the privileged few to see both sides of Harper's life; she hadn't known of their evening plans until Gayle had chosen to inform her.

A delicate muscle moved in her jaw, and she made an attempt to match the other woman's poise, as she remarked, 'Well, you'll be leaving early enough so that you will get into London at a decent hour at least.'

Gayle said quietly, even gently, 'It won't last, you know.'

Nikki's nostrils flared as she sucked in a shocked breath. The older woman had a delicate stiletto touch, pricking her where she would bleed the most. She replied coldly, 'I don't know what you mean.'

Gayle laughed, just a little, just a bare thread of sound, entrapping Nikki in an intimate exchange. 'Of course you do. Harper doesn't suffer fools, so don't play it with me. He's had other relationships.'

'It would be naïve to have expected otherwise,' Nikki bit out. Naturally he had; where else had her lover gained his experience? The thought of him with another woman made her feel nauseous, and she cursed her own vivid imagination.

'They didn't last either,' murmured the blonde, who lifted her head to inspect faultless nails.

Nikki studied the older woman's impenetrable poise without liking, and was proud of steadiness in her voice as she said bluntly, 'Why don't you just get to your point?'

Gayle's green eyes lifted, as did one of her tawny eyebrows, with minute precision. She said softly, 'I've known Harper a good many years. We come from the same background, our families know each other, we have mutual friends. Many of his other liaisons made the same mistake in believing they could hope to change the course of his life. Be careful, Nikki, and guard yourself so you're not hurt too much. As a refreshing little diversion, you're what he wants for now; you're not what he needs.'

The stiletto entered very deep; Nikki wasn't sure, but the wound might just be mortal. She had never before been so vulnerable to another person's casual dismissal, but Gayle had assessed her character perfectly, biding her time over the course of the weekend, waiting for a relaxed moment when barriers were down.

Nikki might not have maintained the level of composure that she did if she hadn't had some kind of warning from Gordon already. Instinctively she sought to wound as she had been wounded, replying drily and with dignity, 'I thank you for your proprietorial interest in my well-being, but it's unnecessary. Harper is lucky to have an old friend so concerned about his needs being met; perhaps one day, when he marries, you will extend the same friendship to his wife.'

The ice queen's façade cracked, and her green eyes glittered hard as jade stone. 'When Harper marries,' said Gayle grittily, 'it will be to someone of his own class who can bear the responsibilities of being his wife, not to some pretentious nobody without distinction!'

Nikki lifted a sleek dark eyebrow in angry parody of Gayle's superior attitude. 'I suspect that Harper will not marry anyone with pretensions, whatever social class they may come from,' she remarked coldly. 'In the meantime, you have watched and waited, while Harper has involved himself in other relationships and the years have gone by so swiftly.'

Gayle spat from between her teeth, 'You will goad him, and he will turn away, and I will be there.'

'Just like always,' murmured Nikki, blue eyes flashing fury and pain, 'picking up the left-overs? Dreaming of a cold and passionless marriage, depending on Harper's discretion as he takes one mistress after another, and you play hostess and work so hard to maintain an acceptable façade to the outside world? Be careful, Gayle, and guard yourself so that you are not hurt too much.'

'He'll never marry you!' snarled the other woman. 'You haven't got what it takes to keep him!'

'I bow to the expert of Harper's needs and desires,' whispered Nikki tautly. 'But I do not recall anyone asking me for an assessment of mine!'

'You're so much in love with him, it's sickening to watch!' Gayle sneered. 'Have you no pride?'

Oh, she had too much, and the hurt had taken over her body so that she trembled from head to toe. If she had been so obvious, then Harper, with the penetrating intelligence that she could never hide from, knew as well.

Harper said from the doorway, 'We're all set.'

Nikki shuddered, for what he might make of the antagonism still raw in the room, for the malignity in Gayle's face that vanished as if it had never been as the other woman's eyes warmed at Harper's appearance.

'I'm ready,' said Gayle as she smiled up at him.

'Good.' He strolled into the room leisurely, his hooded gaze moving from the blonde to Nikki's face, which was an immobile mask. 'Why don't you get your case, then?'

'I'll be right down.'

When Gayle had left the room, Harper dropped his hand lightly on to her shoulder. She could control her expression, but not her shaking body, and she closed her eyes in despair as the masculine fingers tightened like a vice.

'Nikki?' He was sharp, intense. 'What's wrong?'

She said tonelessly, 'Have a good week, Harper. I'll talk to you soon.'

A split-second; she could feel his mind working at computer speed. 'I want you to talk to me now.'

Then her voice shook as well. 'Don't pry. I can't bear it.'

The vice on her shoulder became an expression of utmost gentleness as his fingers lifted to stroke her tight lips, the side of her face. 'Darling,' he said, then he must have reined in whatever emotion had coloured his voice, for his next words were abrupt and to the point, and his hand fell away. 'I'll call you in the week.'

'Fine.' Go away, Harper. Just go away.

She would never know what would have happened had she at last succumbed to looking up at him, for Gayle had returned. In a matter of moments they were gone, and it was none too soon, for Nikki could no longer keep the tears from falling like summer rain.

The next week was the beginning of June, and after travelling back to London with Harper on Sunday evening Nikki went to meet with Peter on Monday morning, and to arrange for some of her art supplies to be sent to Oxford.

She stayed overnight with Harper at the town house in Mayfair, and found that it was surprisingly good to see Duncan Chang again, considering they had only met once. But she realised that Duncan's dark, utterly calm eyes held a fountain of wise strength, from which she drew a vague sense of relief; after all, he looked after Harper very well indeed.

She was stern with herself and kept to her original plan of going back to Oxford early Monday evening, even though she wanted with all her greedy heart to stay another night with Harper. But he was full into the pressures of business, sounding harsh and preoccupied when he spoke to her over the phone at lunchtime, and she refused to become an unwelcome intrusion.

At five o'clock, Harper took a break from his punishing schedule to drive her to Paddington station where she would catch the train to Oxford. It was a strange journey which she would have forgone had she known what it would be like, Harper frowning and silent at the wheel, Nikki staring out of her window at the congested traffic while trying to think of something interesting to say, and tasting the ash-taint of fear at the absence of their weekend's searing rapport.

Perhaps Harper could not sustain what she knew was a phenomenal professional drive and carry on a relationship at the same time; perhaps he was angry with her for some reason; perhaps it was all in her head. Whatever the cause, after she had bought her ticket and he had walked her to the appropriate platform she felt quite miserable as she turned uncertainly to say goodbye to him.

She thought she hid it, but Harper took one look at her face and gave an impatient-sounding groan as he wrapped his arms around her and held her in a bone-crushing grip, and Nikki went wild with humiliation as she thought he was being impatient with her.

'Oh, God, look at the time!' she babbled, twisting her black head away as tears sprang hot to her eyes. 'The next train is going in just a few minutes—I'll have to run!'

When all she wanted was to feel she had the right to stay in the warmth of his arms.

He tightened his hold on her, but only for a moment, and he stepped well away when he released her, his eyes two stones, his jaw like iron. Nikki's heart hurt at the sight; she reached blindly and managed to connect a brushing kiss with his chin, then turned to blunder through the gate. She could not look back. He would be gone, and her foolish heart would hurt all the more, and she railed at herself, Stupid, stupid!

It was only when she had clambered on to the packed train and wedged herself in a standing position between a man and a lady that she realised an odd thing: he hadn't said a single word to her—not in reassurance, in anger, not even in goodbye.

The rest of June went quickly. An entire month, but she took account of it by the weekends. Harper had given her the key to the padlock of the door that led up to her bright new studio, and as soon as her things had been delivered she finished the designs for him in record time, and then turned her efforts towards his painting. Thus began the clock ticking away on her six months' stipulation.

She felt somehow that it was wrong to spend so much time on the subject matter she had chosen, but she couldn't deny herself the obsession. She spent uncounted, unnoticed hours making sketch after sketch and then discarding them, sometimes ripping them to pieces in tempestuous fury at the limitations she sensed in her work for the first time.

And her time with Harper—always afterwards, Nikki would remember that June with an almost unbearable pain, for each weekend flashed upon her with incandescent brilliance. Everything was too vivid, too solidly branded in memory, like the time before an imminent death, and far, far too fleeting. There was a laughter that hurt, a joy so intense that it could kill her, and infrequent but savage arguments. Each confrontation, each lovemaking, every precious tender moment she spent with him was glorious and out of balance.

She tried and tried to figure out how to balance it. She could see Harper's efforts as well—in his conscious reach for patience in the middle of an argument, in his struggle to lighten his frighteningly dark, uncommunicative moods with a smile. Sometimes they nearly achieved synchronisation, and to Nikki those moments were timeless and enchanted, and she would feel so close to serenity, to happiness, that it was almost as sensual as a taste, a touch, a smell. But then, with as little as an inexplicable glance or cryptic remark, the near balance would be destroyed again.

One of those times—oh, how she would always remember it, for it was printed indelibly in her mind. It was the last Sunday afternoon in June, and she and Harper had stayed up late into Saturday night, talking and making love in complete mutual accord.

She had consented that afternoon to play a computer game with Charles, so she went to his room while Harper visited with his mother Helena downstairs.

However, the game with Charles had soon collapsed into giggly, hysterical confusion, for the six-year-old's reaction time was very much faster than hers, and Nikki was woefully inexperienced on a computer keyboard. She had acknowledged a cheerful defeat, chortling to herself at the frank look of pity Charles threw at her, and then, released honourably from her obligation, Nikki had flown with near soundless speed down the staircase to go in search of Harper and his mother.

They had to be in the rear lounge, for they weren't in the front room. She strolled to the open doors as Helena's cultured British accents reached with precise clarity into the hall. 'It's a shame that she cannot see that she is simply unsuitable herself.'

Nikki stopped dead and felt a sharp stab of betrayal. She and Helena had never managed more than a warm politeness, but she genuinely liked Harper's mother, and she had thought that the older woman liked her as well. But over and above mere liking was a tangible bitter scent of disapproval.

She did not move. She projected everything, everything into listening for what Harper would say next. After a moment, harsh and inflexible and like a pronouncement of doom, he said, 'Yes, I know. If I'd known she would be that way, I would never have let it go so far. I just didn't realise how deep her feelings were.'

The betrayal increased into agony; she covered her mouth, though her outcry was soundless, and the pressure in her head was such that she didn't hear what was said next, then Helena asked coolly, 'I suppose breaking off relations will alienate her family as well. It's very disappointing. So what do you intend to do now?'

'I've given Nikki several openings, but she won't even discuss it. She's got the whole thing under lock and key; she's very proud, and it's difficult to get around that.' Harper's laugh sounded angry.

They were discussing her life, her future, her love and happiness, as if she had no right of say or choice. Rage began to beat its reddened fists against the interior of her skull.

'It's clear that you'll have to do something. Things can't go on the way they are,' said Helena, the poise in her voice beginning to reveal fissures of unquiet.

He snapped, 'I've already considered what I'll have to do! In any case, this whole conversation is premature!'

Well. She ought to be thankful for something. At least that did sound as if he hurt a little. Furious and agonised tears splashed down her hands, and she turned to run back upstairs to her room, wishing she hadn't started to cry, wishing she had the ruthlessness to stroll in and confront them both, damn them.

She collided into Charles at the bottom of the stairs, and the boy grabbed hold of her waist. 'Nikki!' he exclaimed, his thin, small face shocked. 'What's wrong?'

She knotted her fingers into his T-shirt and almost shook him as she hissed, 'Don't you mention you saw me, do you hear? Don't you dare breathe a word of this!'

'I—won't!' stammered Charles, half frightened by the violent pain in her. 'I promise! Are you OK? Why are you crying?'

She snarled wordlessly in reply, blue eyes flashing, and hugged herself as if she had nothing else in the world to hold on to. 'Tell your grandmother goodbye for me,' she said from between her teeth, 'tell them I've gone to the studio to work. Tell Harper—tell Harper I'll see him on Friday.'

'Nikki——' The boy reached out one hovering hand but in this he was too young and uncertain, and she was as vicious as a wounded animal.

'Promise me!'

'Yes, all right!'

Now she was hurting him, and he was innocent. She threw her arms around him and whispered into his hair,

'I'm sorry, love. I'm sorry. I'm just very upset right now and need some time to calm down. It'll be our secret, all right?'

He hugged her back, face hidden in her shirt. 'OK.'

In the studio over the garage Nikki threw herself face down on the floor, arms outspread as if she would draw strength from the wooden boards. She did not know how long she lay there. It must have been for ages, for outside the sky darkened.

There was a quick, strong knock on the door at the bottom of the stairs, sounding so loud in the silence that she jumped. She had bolted the lock when she'd entered the studio and now lay very still, listening. It sounded again, and through the distance and the wood she could hear Harper's voice.

She was not surprised. She could not have expected Harper to believe the message she'd sent through Charles, for she had never worked on the weekends while he was there, and she had always made a point of being on hand to say goodbye.

Rebellion seethed a smoky undercurrent inside, and Nikki turned her cheek into the floorboard as she gritted her teeth. She would be damned if she would go downstairs, put on a pretence, cover over what she was really feeling, and watch Harper do the same.

That knock again, more a rattling boom, and a shout ripped out of her throat, 'Go away!'

Her reaction shocked even her, for she had never heard herself sound that way before. After a moment, very calmly and distinctly, Harper said, 'I only wanted to tell you that I'm not going back to London tonight, and I'll see you when you're finished.'

He had fully intended going back, until she had begun to show the unstable hints of some kind of internal stress.

She was so readable; she was so damnably transparent.
Nikki shook with anger directed at both him and herself.
This time she could not run to Harper, so she would
have to try to act with some measure of self-respect instead. It was time she faced some unpalatable facts. She
had loved him too soon and too well, and he would never
love her at all. It was not the end of the world. God, it
only felt as if it was.

Her face contorted and she lifted her fist to pound it
on the floor with such force that she bruised herself up
to the wrist, relinquishing control of the emotions that
ran their ragged, cutting currents, leaving their passage
scored inside her like barren riverbeds that were stony
and dry. At the end of it she was once again in command
of herself, for she had nothing else.

She could not stay there forever. Nikki picked herself
up, dusted off and calmly went down to lock the studio.
It was quite dark outside and deathly quiet so that even
the slightest rustle of wind in the tree leaves and grass
sounded preternaturally loud.

She saw the tall figure leaning against the open French
doors, outlined in golden light that spilled from the rear
lounge and reached long fingers over the green and black
shadowed lawn, and, with an ashen sense of the inevitable, she strolled slowly towards him. She felt as if she
were under a spotlight, laid open to the bone, knowing
without seeing that Harper's eyes took in every aspect
of her appearance and assessed for himself what had
happened to her in the studio.

But her large blue gaze was wry as she came up to
him. She learned so fast and loving him had taught her
a lot, had widened and deepened, and heightened herself
to accommodate all the emotion, the joy, the pain, the
understanding. And now she knew that what he saw in

her he would relate to other things but never guess the truth, for the first real deception had come between them.

What he saw was a face at once so young and so haggard, the eyelids as dark smears, the mouth unfamiliar in bitterness. Her body seemed half abandoned, the spirit that lent such vivacious, darting life to it gone. She moved it now as if it were of no more importance than a childhood doll, already outgrown.

He spoke so simply that she didn't understand why he used such extreme care. 'You didn't paint?'

Nikki turned her head and looked over to the garage. He would have known she hadn't painted, at least after sunset, for there had been no light burning in the windows. 'No. I studied my subject and sulked,' she said, with a flippancy that was vicious beyond self-mockery, another new trait. The light fell on half her face, on the bitter mouth that smiled. 'But then, learning what one can and cannot have is never easy.'

'But must you torment yourself?' he asked her wearily, as if she was tormenting him as well.

She sent him a quick, searching glance and told him thoughtfully, 'In the beginning are sown the seeds of our downfall. Someone said that to me once. A teacher, I think. I don't know if he quoted someone else. I used to wonder why people were so bent on destroying each other, but sometimes now I think that we tear ourselves apart.'

Harper turned to lean against the doorpost too carefully, laying his head back and exposing the colourless, harsh set of his features. In the subtle, interwoven complexities of the man, one of his traits that she had always seen and understood was how overriding his protective instinct was, and in the surest possible way she had stabbed right through him, for the one thing in all the world he could never protect her from was herself.

She had not known that she could be so cruel in her pain. She had not known before she had spoken that she believed what she said.

'I blame myself,' he said, and his mouth twisted. This tall, strong, powerful man was totally vulnerable at that moment, and Nikki's heart twisted as well, for beyond everything else, the moods of the moment and pain of knowledge, she would always love him.

She said, with a tender half-laugh, 'I see you know exactly what I mean.'

The lines radiating from his closed eyes deepened into a wince, and he breathed through his nostrils hard. 'I should never have brought you here,' he said then, savagely. 'I should never have posed that damned painting like a challenge and driven you so hard in your work——'

The ferocious agony lashed her into crying in that light, corrosive voice, 'Tired of me so soon, my dear?'

The expression in his eyes was terrible as they flared open, blazing, eternally dying. He just looked at her and everything bitter and taut and reactive inside Nikki crumbled, and she had nothing left to stand against the lover when she needed the friend so badly.

She asked him in the saddest whisper, her great eyes wide and stripped and vulnerable, 'Harper, how do you stop wanting something you can never have?'

'Oh, Nikki,' he said in a shaken groan, and he held out his arms. She stuffed her fingers against her mouth at the sob that tore through her throat and blundered forwards to be enfolded by the very arms that would some day push her away.

It was impossible, unthinkable. How could one mind contain such a vast difference? How could he reach out and stroke her face in such a gentle caress while knowing what future he had in store for them? How could he kiss her with such feeling, such passion and compassion, and not know a pain so intense as to drive one mad?

She went a little mad herself as he slanted his open mouth over hers with such heedless, violent intensity. She hated him and this desperate physical pleasure, but when he lifted his head she wrapped both arms around his neck wildly and drew him back.

It was her power for now that he came, driven out of himself by what was both lure and plea, and at first she didn't understand what was missing as he lifted her into his arms and carried her through the house.

His long legs flashed swift and unfaltering on the stairs. With each step, Nikki's mind raced further ahead to what awaited them in his room, imagination flooding her with the fiery, compulsive liqueur of desire, but the reality was nothing like she had ever known.

Harper's explosively graceful technique was gone. He was stumbling, his big, naked body uncoordinated as he writhed into her, calling up the deepest kind of atavistic response that was mind-shattering as a whole.

She saw, felt, perceived in splinters. His broken, incoherent murmuring. The sheen of their sweat. Her fingers, clutched in his hair, raking across his back. The way he knew how she would move. The way he knew her. The maelstrom of sexuality that was bigger than both of them, and sucked them whirling and out of control to the climactic centre.

He was the best of all teachers, her lover and her friend. She had known lovemaking as a sensual art, the voluptuary exploration, the rip of unleashed passion, sex in tenderness, laughter, gentleness, and now her education was complete as a lesson in humanity, for this was the bitter-sweet, unendurable lovemaking of despair. She knew the end of it as she knew the limit of her strength.

Afterwards he held her against his gasping chest, and the endless tears streamed out of the corners of her eyes on to her already sweat-soaked skin. She pressed her trembling lips to the frantic pulse-beat in his throat with all the love in her soul, and thought to herself, I will leave him soon.

CHAPTER TEN

HARPER had to leave very early the next morning to make up for his extra night in Oxford, and the sky was barely light when he kissed Nikki gently in farewell. She stirred, more than half asleep, and was unaware of her murmuring sob or how his facial features tightened at the sound. He bent over her, soothing the tangled black hair off her face as he breathed something in her ear that stilled the restless fingers twitching on his empty pillow and smoothed away her frown.

To her it was a lovely dream but like all dreams it had to end, and after it had passed Nikki's sleep became restless again until she woke to a full, bright dawn, and remembered yesterday. She could not bear another love-making like last night, and she could not set aside the despair, so yes, she would have to leave. It was best to go before their relationship descended into further heartbreak and inevitable repudiation.

Everyone had his or her limits; her own she had only just discovered. If she had been more generous, or had more enduring patience, or could have been more hard-headed, perhaps she still could have fought through to win his love, but she simply hadn't the emotional stamina.

There was one concession she could make. She loved and respected Harper so much, and felt such gratitude for the unstinting friendship he had offered to her from the very beginning, that she would tell him face to face that she was leaving. To bolt behind his back seemed cowardly and inappropriate to the good in what they had shared. She owed him more than that, and she owed Charles an explanation for yesterday afternoon.

She had thought to take the train into London in order to talk to Harper that very evening, but just after lunch his secretary rang to tell them that he'd had to fly unexpectedly to the States for a few days.

So she schooled herself to patience. A few days was not so long to wait. And, as she had done with every other emotion she had experienced over the last month, she painted her patience on to the canvas in slow, careful brush strokes.

She told Charles a carefully edited explanation when he got home from school, and that she would have to leave soon; he cried, which moved her very much, and they cuddled and talked late into the evening. From time to time Anne looked in on the two dark heads so close together in the rear lounge. Charles was heavy-eyed and didn't make it to school the next day, but the housekeeper said not a word.

The week passed and still they heard nothing from Harper until Nikki thought anxiously late Thursday afternoon that he surely had to come home the next day. She didn't know if she could wait any longer; for each hour that went by, a little more of her resolve trickled away.

That week she finished work when Charles came home from school, so that she could spend as much time as possible with him, and as he helped her pack supplies into the boxes in the studio on Friday they both heard the hard crunch of car tyres on gravel and looked at each other.

'He's home,' said Nikki and Charles nodded, his head downbent. They both knew it was the end.

They did not know it would be something else. Nikki followed the boy downstairs and out of the garage on leaden limbs, and as they walked around the corner of the house they both halted in surprise at the sight of two men climbing out of the Jaguar, not one.

The driver was Harper, of course, grim with exhaustion and casually dressed in jeans and shirt, but Nikki's blue glance only touched him briefly on the way to inspecting the other, younger man.

The two standing by the Jaguar saw her. She took a step forward and her heart thudded. 'Johnny?'

Her brother's face lit up. He said, his eyes laughing, loving, 'Hello, stranger.'

'Johnny!' Her eyes and voice blazed. She ran and did not know it until she hurtled into her brother's arms, who swung her around just as he used to when they were younger, and she was babbling and laughing at him all at once.

Johnny stopped, and she caught her breath and managed to articulate her first sensible questions. 'What are you doing here? How do you know Harper? Did you get your birthday present?'

'Stop!' he exclaimed. They were grinning maniacally at each other, but then her brother sobered until he wore a look that was every bit as stubborn as hers could be, and he cupped her small, upturned face in his hands as he told her, 'Yes, I got your present, thanks very much, and, as for knowing Harper, he showed up at my apartment on Tuesday evening and introduced himself. As for what I'm doing here, I've come to try to take you back home with me if I can.'

What Harper had done was at once so simple and yet so staggering that she would have fallen had Johnny not gripped her so tightly. She could not believe the cruel efficiency of it.

She cast one anguished glance over her shoulder at Harper, who stood silently watching them some ten feet away, his hands in his pockets. Then Charles was beside his uncle, exclaiming in pained incomprehension, 'I don't understand! You brought that man here to take Nikki away? But she was already going to leave!'

Nikki saw Harper's eyes go dead.

She didn't understand him at all, not any more, not when he could have done something like this to her. She hardly knew she was shaking like a leaf until Johnny forcibly turned her head around to him and said, clear and steady, 'Nikki, we have to talk now. Can we go somewhere private?'

She couldn't see the expression on her brother's face, for her eyes were blinded with tears. 'Yes,' she choked, making a desperate attempt to pull her shattered self together. 'The studio's empty. We can go there if you like.'

'Where is it?' Johnny wiped away the wetness spilling down her cheeks matter-of-factly.

'Around the side, over the garage. I'll—I'll take you.' In spite of her words, it was he who led her gently from the scene, for she was in a state of deep shock. Her wavering footsteps automatically guided them to the garage, and somehow they climbed the stairs, though she did not remember doing so. Nikki stood in the centre of the spacious room that smelled of paint and turpentine, and she was lost.

But Johnny wasn't, as he turned to her and said urgently, 'Nikki, everyone is concerned about you. Mother and Karle want to know when you're going to come home. I want to know. I miss the sister who was my one playmate through all the world, and I want a chance to get better acquainted with the beautiful young woman you've grown into. Haven't you had enough of living abroad yet?'

She'd heard the same speech, in different ways from various members of the family, ever since she had graduated from university three years ago, and hardly paid attention to it. Instead she focused on the one point that brought her so much pain and whispered, 'How could Harper do this to me? If he wanted me to leave, why didn't he just say so?'

Johnny's expression flickered. For long moments her brother was silent. Everything was silent. There was no wind on that sunny day, no sounds of traffic so far back from the road, just the occasional call of a bird; she used to think it was so peaceful.

Then her brother said very quietly, 'Nikki, I can't lie to you. Harper deserves better than that. When he stopped by in New York, he introduced himself as the man who had fallen in love with you and intended to ask you to marry him. It was quite a shock. Coming to England was my idea. We had no idea that you were thinking of setting down roots here. Even though he knew I would try to take you back to the States, he still allowed me to travel back with him. I respect him very much; I don't think I would have had that kind of strength.'

Nikki's head came up. Incredulity, a terrible hope, and a kind of fury shone in her eyes, and, even though she was only a slight, small woman, suddenly the airy studio seemed barely capable of containing her. 'He said that?' she whispered.

Johnny's hazel eyes widened in awe at the change in her, then darkened with the beginnings of regret. But still he tried, moving quickly to place his hands on her shoulders. 'Listen to me, Nikki! Please come back home, even if only for a while. Give yourself a chance to get reacquainted with everyone—if you settle here, the distance between us will become permanent——'

It was like trying to cage a wildfire, like reaching for the moon. Nikki leaned forward, grabbed Johnny's shirt and cried, *'Did he say all that?'*

Her brother closed his eyes and whispered, 'Yes.'

She vibrated like a musical instrument, audible lambency, vitally transformed, but for him she tried the impossible and managed to restrain the roaring, swelling flood. 'I will show you the woman I have grown into,' said Nikki, stepping back in a light, fluid dance that took her to a corner where a large covered canvas sat on an easel, and with one sweep of her arm she unveiled the unfinished picture beneath it.

Johnny moved to look, and stopped, and stared.

The flood was ungovernable and it swept her away; she whirled and cried melodiously, 'I have to go talk to him! Oh, Johnny—Johnny, I love you, but going back to the States isn't going home! I'm sorry!'

Her brother didn't answer. He didn't need to. Looking at the picture, he already knew he had lost.

Nikki flew down the stairs with lightning speed. 'I don't understand,' Charles had said. She sprinted across the lawn, hurtled through the back door into the kitchen. Anne looked around from the sink and opened her mouth to say something, but Nikki ran past and never saw her. 'You brought that man here to take Nikki away?' Charles had said, and with all her heart and soul she cried, No, no!

She stumbled to the rear lounge, but it was empty, and she flew from room to room in a frantic whirlwind, searching for him. He wasn't anywhere.

'*But she was already going to leave!*'

The terrible look in his eyes.

She was gasping in her exertion and distress as she ran up the stairs, down the hall. What if he had left, where would he have gone, what would he do? Could she get him to listen to her?

She threw open his bedroom door. It crashed resoundingly against the wall, and across the room Harper sat doubled over on the edge of his bed. He lifted his head from his hands. Only for an instant did she get a glimpse of that unguarded, lonely expression, the face of a man desolate and grieving, the utter bleakness of a conqueror defeated.

Then it was gone as if it had never happened, replaced by sardonicism, remoteness, impregnable ice. He said almost casually, 'So when do you leave?'

'Damn you!' she panted, furious and aching and so in love with him that she could have died from it. She strode violently into the room and stopped distracted in the middle of it, holding her hands stiff and clenched at her side. 'Will it always be this way between us?'

She had never seen Harper's dark eyes so hard and repellent. He said cuttingly, 'Spare me your wild accusations. I was under the impression that there was no more "us".'

'Spare you?' she cried, nearly incoherent with the need to break through to him. 'I will not! You can never be satisfied! You always have to push me away! Why on earth would I want to spare you?'

Harper surged to his feet, his body in eruptive, athletic motion that had the deadly speed of a striking snake.

She knew fear then, for the ice was gone and so at last was all restraint. He said savagely, 'If you've come here for some kind of blood-letting, by God I'll throw you out of my house!'

'Do it!' she shrieked in uncontrollable rage as she lifted her fists to her forehead. 'That won't stop me loving you! You'll have to cut out my heart!'

The whiplash of that resounded in the room. Harper shuddered, an oak tree brought under the woodman's axe. In Nikki's head ran the awful image of him laying his hands on her, only to push her violently away, out the door, out of his life, and she couldn't survive it. Overwhelmed, she turned to flee blindly, only to miss the open doorway and run into the post.

In groaning, wrenching torment, Harper cried, 'Why are you leaving me?'

She leaned her face against the wood, her mouth bowing open in a sob. 'I was going to leave before you sent me away!'

'Send you away?' She sensed him coming up behind her, and shrank away in a gasping flinch. Then his hands were running unsteadily over her back, her shoulders, her neck and hair. 'Shh, oh, shh, darling,' he whispered. 'No. No. How could you think I could send you away? I don't even know if I can let you go.'

But, no matter how he tried to gentle her, the storm was unleashed and she shook and sobbed as if she would never stop. 'But I heard you talking to Helena on Sunday, and she said—she said—that I was unsuitable, that I——'

'Dear God.' He turned her, and gathered her close, and bound her against his chest with arms tighter than steel, cradling her head into the hollow of his neck, bowing his whole body around her.

'Nikki, Nikki, if that's what you thought, you couldn't have heard it all! Don't cry like that; it breaks my heart to hear it—listen to me! My mother and I were talking about Gayle, not you! When I took Gayle back to London last month, I knew something was wrong, but you refused to talk about it, so I questioned her instead. She told me—well, enough to get the gist of what had happened between you. I'd had no idea that she had entertained such hopes for a relationship between us, or that she could be so bitchy. I was explaining to my mother why I had to terminate my friendship with Gayle, because her relations with Gayle's family had become strained.'

'But she—she said that things couldn't continue, and you said you would have to do something—I don't remember what!' she said, muffled in the bare, throbbing warmth of his neck. She barely knew what she said. All her starving senses were focused on the surety of his hold on her, the animal comfort of his body, the hungry tenderness of his hand cupping her head, and her arms slid around the steady column of his waist.

He sighed. She felt and heard it. 'Stupid child,' said Harper with angry gentleness. 'I'd just finished telling her of the strain Gayle had put between you and me. I wanted you to come to me yourself with it, but you're probably the most stubborn creature imaginable. She was concerned for you, that's all.'

'Well, you could have told me,' she said shakily. 'You seemed to have told everyone else in the world.'

He took her head and pulled her back so that he could look down into her face, and all the love in his voice was there tenfold in his dark eyes which were lit inside like a beacon. 'How could I tell you?' he asked tenderly. 'We happened on it too fast, we were racing out of control. You had so much to cope with. Your career, that vicious attack on you. I was the first man to make love to you, and for all I knew you were caught in some sexual infatuation and could have mistaken it for love. The fact that we became friends as well only seemed to complicate the issue.'

'No,' she whispered, shaking her head, feeling her hair slide along the palms of his hands. 'Our friendship made it so clear. I'm not just in love with you, I love you, with everything inside me, heart and body and soul.'

All the residual harshness in his face melted, leaving him clear-eyed and young again. 'I knew I loved you that Friday afternoon when I walked into Peter's office and you looked at me with such shaken wonder, with all your innocent heart full in those beautiful blue eyes. But then,' Harper said wryly, 'I was fighting it for all I was worth—a sorry struggle, for I was fighting myself. I wanted you so badly, it was like an ache in my gut, but, damn it, I have so many demands on my time— people, and work, and Charles, while you——'

'Will either be your deliriously happy wife, or very miserable without you,' she said, her face misting with such wistfulness that he caught his breath and bent to kiss her softened, offered lips. 'Oh, Harper, Johnny said you intended to ask me to marry you, but already you're putting up barriers again,' she groaned against his mouth. 'If you let anything else come between us, I'll never forgive you.'

'No,' he murmured, running his fingers along her cheekbones, down to her jaw, lightly over the slim vulnerability of her neck. 'Nothing else between us. I cannot deny this, nor you, who are so wise and witty and young. The way you know me, and fit so close in my heart and to my body, it would be like denying part of myself.'

She caught his hands and kissed them. 'I'm sorry about Charles,' she said softly.

Harper laughed quietly. 'I take it you two had some heart-to-hearts while I was gone. God, I can't leave you alone together for long! Either one of you would only get the other into trouble. The scamp told me he would never forgive me if I took you out of his life.'

'Oh, no!' Nikki closed her eyes, both appalled and touched. 'I'd better go talk to him soon. Harper, about Johnny——'

His chest moved in a harsh, silent laugh and he leaned his forehead against hers. 'Bad timing,' he said. 'Bad, bad timing. But, as I was already in New York for business, it seemed only reasonable to look your family up and make a statement of intent, so that they'd finally become resigned to the possibility that you might never go back to the States again. Then, to my horror, your brother insisted on coming back to England with me. My heart was in my throat for the entire trip. I'd meant to talk with you first and explain things, but circumstances backfired on me.'

'Oh, God,' she sighed, and kissed him repentantly. 'If there hadn't been so many misunderstandings, it would have been fine.'

'Your family may never forgive me,' said Harper, stroking her lips with the tips of his fingers. 'Your brother is a very determined young man. I like him tremendously.'

'Nuts to my family—they're interfering busybodies. Johnny likes you as well,' murmured Nikki, and a thought struck her so that she began to laugh. 'Oh, let's add to the list. Peter will have a fit when he finds out. He's most upset about this painting I'm doing for you. We've cut out his position.'

Harper said toughly, though his face was lit with a smile, 'He'll come to terms with it. But about that infernal painting. Please don't torture yourself any more over it, my love. For God's sake, it isn't worth it.'

'What?' she replied, looking at him blankly, and then she remembered. 'Heavens, I wasn't talking about the painting on Sunday night. I was talking about you. The painting is the best thing I've ever done.'

'Are you sure?' he asked, even as relief spread over him. With every barrier peeled away, he appeared lighter, until he almost looked like a different man. A complete man, she thought, as she studied him with love. The two halves of his personality were finally melded together, no longer in conflict. 'I'm so pleased. When can I see it?'

She wrinkled her nose at him. 'When it's finished, and not a moment before! Otherwise you'll spoil the surprise.'

The unpredictable slant of his eyebrows became more pronounced. 'You're going to make me wait?'

His mouth was so sexy when he held it like that, the mobility in taut control, the hint of sternness that would melt into such giving pleasure. She tilted up her small chin and her eyes sparkled as she told him challengingly, 'For some things, yes. It'll do you good. You get your own way too often, if you ask me.'

The delicious bite was back again, the eternal pursuit and conquest, the spice of sexuality that flavoured their repartee, heightening her awareness to a fever pitch, as she knew a reawakening of the soul-shaking excitement. He narrowed his eyes speculatively and murmured, 'I wonder if I could make you change your mind?'

She bared her teeth at him and snapped, 'Not likely!'

'I could give it a good try,' he growled, and the dark hunger in his gaze lowered to her mouth as if he couldn't help himself. The air began to crackle. He snapped the full swell of her lower lip with one fingernail, raking it gently as he whispered, 'Your lips are like crushed velvet.'

The stuffing left her legs in a whoosh, but she jerked her head away, stepped back and advised him with cool, taunting insouciance, 'Hold that thought. In the meantime, I shall go down to visit with my brother and talk to Charles. The poor boy must be feeling quite neglected.'

Thoroughly roused, Harper caught her by the hips and dragged her back to him, torso to torso, and he gave her a tight, predatory smile. 'Oh, no, you're not.'

'Oh, yes, I am!' she flashed. Their eyes collided and sizzled, and Harper brought down his opened mouth like an avalanche when she whispered just one evocative word. 'Later.'

They both enjoyed the conflagration.

In the end, they had all underestimated Nicole Ashton-Meyer—the gossip, society and fashion columnists, Harper's business associates, and all the wedding guests. Despite her youth the vivid, dashing woman who appeared on her brother's arm and started up the aisle bore not the slightest resemblance to a blushing, demure bride.

Gordon as best man dug his elbow painfully into Harper's side, who turned and began to shake with laughter. Her wedding dress that she'd kept such a secret was white, shoulderless, and figure-hugging down to her knees where the skirt flared extravagantly to the floor. Underneath the jaunty tilt of the most delicious, outrageous, frothy hat exploding with white feathers Nikki's blue eyes peeped at him naughtily.

She practically flounced up the aisle, and when Johnny very carefully gave her away, his face stiff with suppressed mirth, she whispered desperately out of the corner of her mouth to Harper, 'For God's sake, don't let go! The hem got caught on a nail, and I keep tripping over it! If I fall now, I won't be able to get back up because the dress is so tight!'

His control over his expression was awesome. Harper whispered soothingly as he clutched her in an iron grip, 'Don't worry, love, I've got you.'

All the audience saw was a very private murmured exchange, and then the groom tenderly took hold of his bride's arm, and Harper Beaumont's associates, rivals and outright enemies began to feel very smug at how possessive he looked. His lovely bride would mellow out that tempered steel personality; it was clear that he was absolutely besotted with her, and they all began to predict a relaxation of that famous Beaumont ruthlessness.

But then the minister asked her if she would take the groom for her lawful wedded husband, and the dreadful scamp of a bride hesitated for far too long, tilted up her chin and gave the marital catch of the decade a slow, considering look before she answered an affirmative. And the hearts of all Harper's associates sank in unison at the brilliant, predatory look that hardened his handsome features into an expression they well recognised, and they knew to a man that they'd been guilty of wishful thinking.

The reception was glorious. Even though the howl of frigid December winds whipped shrieking and bleak outside, the hall in London was filled with warmth and golden light like a spell of enchantment, intoxicating, atmospheric champagne.

The happiness was infectious. Charles sipped at some stolen champagne and beleaguered Duncan Chang with his inebriated presence, but the slight man bore up well under the pressure, and on that night his rare, beautiful smile was ever-present. Helena Beaumont held gracious court at one end of the hall and it was observed that, while the bride's family had a certain air of resignation about them, relations between two of the world's wealthiest families appeared good.

The indefatigable Peter Bellis handed out business cards to anyone who was willing to take them, but could not resist several speculative glances toward a huge covered canvas that was propped on an easel in one corner.

It was Nikki's wedding present to Harper, the painting finished just a few weeks ago, and it was to be unveiled later in the evening. But for the moment there were speeches to be made, and supper, and the cutting of the wedding cake, and dancing.

After the formal photographs had been taken, Nikki had removed her hat, for the hall was very warm. She collared her mother for a few private moments in the cloakroom, and between the two women they had pinned up her dragging hem. Now her happiness was so intense and complete that she was everywhere, darting from group to group like a hummingbird. What sang through her mind over and over were the softly murmured words Harper had spoken in her ear just after the ceremony when they had become husband and wife.

He had pulled her close, his dark eyes insatiable, and as he bent his leonine grey head down to her he whispered, 'By your own choice you've committed yourself and I will never let you go. I love you too selfishly.'

In the end the man in him had overcome the friend who would have given her whatever she desired, even her freedom, no matter what the cost was to himself. But the change in Harper was irrelevant, almost trivial, for Nikki had all she had ever wanted and he was standing right before her with his magnificent heart in his eyes. The change was almost trivial, but not quite, for by letting himself reach out and take what he wanted from her she hoped fervently that he would never again think to draw away.

But still the ghost of anxiety lingered in the clear, wide gaze that she turned up to his handsome face. The last six months had been almost too perfect, and she could not suppress her superstitious fear that their stormy beginning had scarred in her. Nikki whispered back, and did not hear the pleading in her voice, 'Then you must hold on to me very tight.'

Her patient husband was very wise. He saw and understood the faint shadow in her blue eyes better than she did. But, just as he had taught her all the consummative joys in lovemaking, he would teach her about security and faithfulness, and constancy, and reaffirm the lesson all the years of his life, until that last faint shadow had gone forever.

He did not tell her that. She would grow to know it for herself. Instead he had enfolded her in his arms and said as a tender promise, 'Always.'

He was coming after her now. Wicked glee bubbled up inside her as she fled throughout the crowded hall, parrying quips and exchanging pleasantries, while keeping one laughing eye trained behind her at Harper's elegant, tall figure restrained from an all-out chase by social convention.

She watched as yet another acquaintance hampered his progress, and his intent face grew tight with frustration as he threw her one hard glance before turning with an urbane smile to the man beside him. Nikki came up to her mother and Helena, and chatted for a few moments until she saw Harper break free from the other man, his handsome expression eloquent in relief. She laughed out loud.

'You must excuse me,' Nikki told the two women hurriedly. 'Harper's trying to catch me; I've got to run!'

And off she went again, while Mrs Heissenger stared in astonishment at her son-in-law's tall, aggressive form in full hunt, and said, 'She will try him too far.'

'On the contrary,' said Helena in thoughtful wisdom, catching sight of the hungry, reckless look in Harper's eyes as he watched his incorrigible wife, 'she will try him just far enough.'

He caught her at last, but then she let him, and as the orchestra began to play he whirled her around the great open expanse of the dance-floor in a sweeping waltz, while the whole crowded room stopped to watch. Nikki didn't even feel her feet touch the floor. All her attention was focused on the wild, sexy man whose eloquent eyes played a music of their own just for her.

The waltz died away but their music didn't stop. It swelled and rebounded on itself, and crashed in symphonic crescendo. Through it ran the unsteady strains of her uncertainty, until she had to ask him, 'Will you forgive me?'

Harper smiled in incomprehension, fascinated by every change in her mood. 'For what?' he asked, touching the pulsation at her throat with long, caressing fingers.

'For the picture I painted,' she whispered from a re-stricted throat, and she licked her lips, which had gone dry.

Harper's body went still, the indulgent light-heartedness fading from his lean face. With one sharp, frowning glance into her apprehensive eyes, he stepped back, his arms falling away, and he turned to stride across the empty expanse of the dance-floor towards the covered canvas. The wedding guests made way for him, all eyes trained on him, and Nikki left standing alone.

Harper reached the large picture, grasped the cloth with one hand and threw it away. A sighing murmur rippled through the crowd as the painting was revealed. In one corner, Peter Bellis made a sound of ecstasy and loss.

Nikki could not see Harper's face and she clasped her cold hands together in spasmodic anxiety. He seemed to stand forever in that stark, rigid posture, staring at the portrait of himself. She knew the terrible sense of ex-posure he must be feeling, as she knew her own, for the painting was everything.

Sober and light; exquisite sensuality in every brush stroke of graceful hands and ruthless mouth; tenderness and compassion and hard-stamped features; longing and grief and the threshold of joy contained in the im-mutable expression of those dark painted eyes. The portrait was everything he was—timeless and irre-futable—but, most revealing of all, it was a tran-scendent statement of all her love and depth of understanding.

Nikki approached his rock-like graven figure tenta-tively, hoping, praying. She reached his side and stopped, and though he did not look around he must have known she was there, for he said from the back of his throat,

'You were right. It is the best thing you have ever done. It deserved to be shown.'

But his face and words told her nothing; she did not know whether he spoke in accusation or agreement, until he turned his glittering, proud, moist eyes on to her and she saw how deeply moved he was. He whispered, 'Thank you.'

She moved and smiled radiantly, and her world which had stopped began to turn again.

Time sped fleetingly, until, by unspoken consent, Harper and Nikki went to change clothes. Off came the splendid pageantry; he dressed in trousers and sweater and leather jacket, she donned jeans and the Harvard sweatshirt her brother Johnny had given her. They had to hurry, otherwise they would be late for their plane flight which would take them far south to the sunlit Nile for a two-week cruise, and as they came back out again their family and closest friends gathered around to say goodbye.

Nikki's head spun from the flurry of hurried hugs. Her mother whispered simply, 'Stay happy, darling.' Johnny crushed her ribs. Helena talked quietly to her son. Charles almost knocked her over and planted a clumsy kiss somewhere in the region of her nose, and Gordon gave her a naughty wink.

She withstood it all in a dream-like trance that was blown away by priceless reality when Harper turned to her at last with his heart-stopping smile, and asked, 'Are you ready?'

Their loved ones bore witness when she gave his own earlier promise back to him, with a transparent generosity that enriched them all with a share in that most private commitment, as she whispered, 'Always.'

Relive the romance...
Harlequin®is proud to bring you

A new collection of three complete novels every month. By the most requested authors, featuring the most requested themes.

Available in October:

DREAMSCAPE

They're falling under a spell!
But is it love—or magic?

Three complete novels in one special collection:

GHOST OF A CHANCE by Jayne Ann Krentz
BEWITCHING HOUR by Anne Stuart
REMEMBER ME by Bobby Hutchinson

Available wherever Harlequin books are sold.

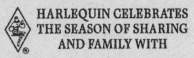